Citizenship Papers

Also by Wendell Berry

CITIZENSHIP PAPERS

WENDELL BERRY

SHOEMAKER & HOARD
Washington, DC

Library of Congress Cataloging-in-Publication Data is available.
ISBN: 1-59376-000-0

FIRST PRINTING

Jacket and text design by Gopa & Ted2, Inc.
Printed in the United States of America on acid-free paper

 Shoemaker & Hoard
A Division of Avalon Publishing Group Incorporated
Distributed by Publishers Group West

10 9 8 7 6 5 4 3 2 1

Most of these essays were written as speeches, as most of my essays in previous collections have been. Their subjects vary somewhat, but all of them come from my continuing interest in the requirements of neighborliness and stewardship, true security and true patriotism. Some themes and ideas therefore are repeated throughout. To the extent that apology is needed for this, I apologize.

I am grateful to Tanya Berry and Tanya Charlton, who have typed and retyped these pages, giving me in the process much useful advice, not all of it literary.

I need also to thank Charlie Sing and Richard Strohman for their generous instruction on issues of science, but they did not take me to raise and are in no way responsible for my faults.

For many clarifications I am indebted to my brother, John Marshall Berry, Jr. To him, to my children, and to my agrarian friends Gene Logsdon, Maurice Telleen, and Wes Jackson, I am grateful for the companionship that gives courage and enforces care.

My thanks go also to the editors of the following periodicals, in which versions of these essays first were printed: *Orion, The Land Report, Shambala Sun, The Amicus Journal, The Natural Farmer, The Farmer's Pride, The Progressive, Sustain, The Oxford American,* and *Sierra.*

The essay here entitled "The Total Economy" has been previously published a number of times as "The Idea of a Local Economy." And "Conservationist and Agrarian" appeared in *Sierra* as "For Love of the Land."

The last section of "The Whole Horse" was first published as "Hope" in *Fatal Harvest,* edited by Andrew Kimbrell, published by Island Press.

Three of these essays—"Thoughts in the Presence of Fear," "The Idea of a Local Economy" ("The Total Economy"), and "In Distrust of Movements"—were published as *In the Presence of Fear* by The Orion Society.

Norman MacAfee copyedited my manuscript carefully and kindly, and I am grateful to him for that.

Finally, I thank my dear friends Shoemaker and Hoard, who are necessary to me both as a Company and as company.

Were it not that I am passionately fond of the contours
of my country, I should not be here.
—Cézanne

And through covetousness shall they with feigned words
make merchandise of you . . .
—II Peter 2:3

I dedicate this volume to the memory of John Adams, Samuel Adams, Josiah Bartlett, Carter Braxton, Charles Carroll, Samuel Chase, Abraham Clark, George Clymer, William Ellery, William Floyd, Benjamin Franklin, Elbridge Gerry, Button Gwinnett, Lyman Hall, John Hancock, Benjamin Harrison, John Hart, Joseph Hewes, Thomas Heyward, Jr., William Hooper, Stephen Hopkins, Francis Hopkinson, Samuel Huntington, Thomas Jefferson, Francis Lightfoot Lee, Richard Henry Lee, Francis Lewis, Philip Livingston, Thomas Lynch, Jr., Thomas McKean, Arthur Middleton, Lewis Morris, Robert Morris, John Morton, Thomas Nelson, Jr., William Paca, Robert Treat Paine, John Penn, George Read, Caesar Rodney, George Ross, Benjamin Rush, Edward Rutledge, Roger Sherman, James Smith, Richard Stockton, Thomas Stone, George Taylor, Matthew Thornton, George Walton, William Whipple, William Williams, James Wilson, John Witherspoon, Oliver Wolcott, and George Wythe.

Contents

CITIZENSHIP PAPERS

A Citizen's Response to "The National Security Strategy of the United States of America"

The constituent parts of a state are obliged to hold their public faith with each other, and with all those who derive any serious interest under their engagements, as much as the whole state is bound to keep its faith with separate communities. Otherwise competence and power would soon be confounded, and no law be left but the will of a prevailing force.

—Edmund Burke, *On the Revolution in France*

America! America!
God mend thine every flaw,
Confirm thy soul in self control,
Thy liberty in law.

—Katharine Lee Bates, "America the Beautiful"

To seek for peace by way of war is the same as to seek for chastity by way of fornication.

—Anonymous theologian of the first century

I.

THE NEW "National Security Strategy" published by the White House in September 2002, if carried out, would amount to a radical revision of the political character of our nation. This document was conceived in reaction to the terrorist attacks of September 11, 2001. Its central and most significant statement is this:

> While the United States will constantly strive to enlist the support of the international community, we will not hesitate to act alone, if necessary, to exercise our right of self-defense by acting preemptively against such terrorists . . .

A democratic citizen, properly uneasy, must deal here first of all with the question, Who is this "we"? It is not the "we" of the Declaration of Independence, which referred to a small group of signatories bound by the conviction that "governments [derive] their just powers from the consent of the governed." And it is not the "we" of the Constitution, which refers to "*the people* [my emphasis] of the United States."

Because of what is implied by the commitment to act alone and preemptively, this "we" of the new strategy can refer only to the president. It is a royal "we." A head of state, preparing to act alone in starting a preemptive war, will need to justify his intention by secret information, and will need to plan in secret and execute his plan without forewarning. A preemptive attack widely known and discussed, as in a democratic polity, would risk being preempted by a preemptive attack by the other side. The idea of a government acting alone in preemptive war is inherently undemocratic, for it does not require or even permit the president to obtain the consent of the governed. As a policy, this new strategy depends on the acquiescence of a public kept fearful and ignorant, subject to manipulation by the executive power, and on the compliance of an intimidated and office-dependent legislature. Even within the narrow logic of warfare, there is a substantial difference between a defensive action, for which the reason would be publicly known, and a preemptive or aggressive action, for which the reason would be known only by a few at the center of power. The responsibilities of the president obviously are not mine, and so I hesitate to doubt absolutely the necessity of governmental secrecy. But I feel no hesitation in saying that to the extent that a government is secret, it cannot be democratic or its people free. By this new doctrine, the president alone may start a war against any nation at any time, and with no more forewarning than preceded the Japanese attack on Pearl Harbor.

Would-be participating citizens of a democratic nation, unwilling to have their consent coerced or taken for granted, therefore have no choice but to remove themselves from the illegitimate constraints of this "we" in as immediate and public a way as possible.

But as this document and its supporters insist, we have now entered a new era when acts of war may be carried out not only by nations and "rogue nations," but also by individuals using weapons of mass destruction, and this requires us to give up some measure of freedom in return for some increase of security. The lives of every one of us may at any time be in jeopardy.

Even so, we need to ask: What does real security require of us? What does true patriotism require of us? What does freedom require of us?

The alleged justification for this new strategy is the recent emergence in the United States of international terrorism. But why the events of September 11, 2001, horrifying as they were, should have called for a radical new investiture of power in the executive branch is not clear.

"The National Security Strategy" defines terrorism as "premeditated, politically motivated violence perpetrated against innocents." This is truly a distinct kind of violence, but it is a kind old and familiar, even in the United States. All that was really new about the events of September 11, 2001, was that they raised the scale of such violence to that of "legitimate" modern warfare.

To imply by the word "terrorism" that this sort of terror is the work exclusively of "terrorists" is misleading. The "legitimate" warfare of technologically advanced nations likewise is premeditated, politically motivated violence perpetrated against innocents. The distinction between the *intention* to perpetrate violence against innocents, as in "terrorism," and the *willingness* to do so, as in "war," is not a source of comfort. We know also that modern war, like ancient war, often involves intentional violence against innocents.

A more correct definition of "terrorism" would be this: violence perpetrated unexpectedly without the authorization of a national government. Violence perpetrated unexpectedly *with* such authorization is not "terrorism" but "war." If a nation perpetrates violence officially—whether to bomb an enemy airfield or a hospital—it is not guilty of "terrorism." But there is no need to hesitate over the difference between "terrorism" and any violence or threat of violence that is terrifying. "The National Security Strategy" wishes to cause "terrorism" to be seen "in the same light as slavery, piracy, or genocide"—but not in the same light as war. It accepts and affirms the legitimacy of war.

This document concedes that "we are menaced less by fleets and armies than by catastrophic technologies in the hands of the embittered few." And yet our government, with our permission, continues to manufacture, stockpile, and trade in these catastrophic technologies, including nuclear, chemical, and biological weapons. In nuclear or biological warfare, in which we know we cannot limit effects, how do we distinguish our enemies from our friends—or our enemies from ourselves? Does this not bring us exactly to the madness of terrorists who kill themselves in order to kill others?

The official definition of "terrorism," then, is far too exclusive if we seriously wish to free the world of the terrors induced by human violence. But let us suppose that our opposition to terror could be justly or wisely limited to a "war against terrorism." How effective might such a war be?

The war against terrorism is not, strictly speaking, a war against nations, even though it has already involved international war in Afghanistan and presidential threats against other nations. This is a war against "the embittered few"—"thousands of trained terrorists"—who are "at large" among many thousands and even millions of others who are, in the language of this document, "innocents," and thus deserving of our protection.

Hunting these terrorists down will be like combing lice out of a head of hair. Unless we are willing to kill innocents in order to kill the guilty—unless we are willing to blow our neighbor's head off, or blow our own head off, to get rid of the lice—the need to be lethal will be impeded constantly by the need to be careful. Because of the inherent difficulties and because we must suppose a new supply of villains to be always in the making, we can expect the war on terrorism to be more or less endless, endlessly costly and endlessly supportive of a thriving bureaucracy.

Unless, that is, we should become willing to ask why, and to do something about the causes. Why do people become terrorists? Such a question is often dismissed as evidence of "liberal softness" toward malefactors. But that is not necessarily the case. Such a question may also arise from the recognition that problems have causes. There is, however, no acknowledgment in "The National Security Strategy" that terrorism might have a cause that could possibly be discovered and possibly remedied. "The embittered few," it seems, are merely "evil."

II.

Much of the obscurity of our effort so far against terrorism originates in the now official idea that the enemy is evil and that we are (therefore) good, which is the precise mirror image of the official idea of the terrorists.

The epigraph of Part III of the "National Security Strategy" contains this sentence from President Bush's speech at the National Cathedral on September 14, 2001: "But our responsibility to history is already clear: to answer these attacks and rid the world of evil." A government, committing its nation to rid the world of evil, is assuming necessarily that it and its nation are good.

But the proposition that anything so multiple and large as a nation can be good is an insult to common sense. It is also dangerous, because it precludes any attempt at self-criticism or self-correction; it precludes public dialogue. It leads us far indeed from the traditions of religion and democracy that are intended to measure and so to sustain our efforts to be good. "There is none good but one, that is, God," Christ said. Also: "He that is without sin among you, let him first cast a stone at her." And Thomas Jefferson justified general education by the obligation of citizens to be critical of their government: "for nothing can keep it right but their own vigilant *and distrustful* [my emphasis] superintendence." An inescapable requirement of true patriotism, love for one's land, is a vigilant distrust of any determinative power, elected or unelected, that may preside over it.

And so it is not without reason or precedent that a would-be participating citizen should point out that in addition to evils originating abroad and supposedly correctable by catastrophic technologies in "legitimate" hands, we have an agenda of domestic evils, not only those that properly self-aware humans can find in their own hearts, but also several that are indigenous to our history as a nation: issues of economic and social justice, and issues related to the continuing and worsening maladjustment between our economy and our land.

There are kinds of violence that have nothing directly to do with unofficial or official warfare but are accepted as normal to our economic life. I mean such things as toxic pollution, land destruction, soil erosion, and the destruction of biological diversity, and of the degradation of ecological supports of agriculture. To anybody with a normal concern for health and sanity, these "externalized costs" are terrible and are terrifying.

I don't wish to make light of the threats and dangers that now confront us. There can be no doubt of the reality of terrorism as defined and understood by "The National Security Strategy," or of the seriousness of our situation, or of our need for security. But frightening as all this is, it does not relieve us of the responsibility to be as intelligent, principled, and practical as we can be. To rouse the public's anxiety about foreign terror while ignoring domestic terror, and to fail to ask if these terrors are in any way related, is wrong.

It is understandable that we should have reacted to the attacks of September 11, 2001, by curtailment of civil rights, by defiance of laws, and by resort to overwhelming force, for those actions are the ready products of fear and hasty thought. But they cannot protect us against the destruction of our own land by ourselves. They cannot protect us against the selfishness, wastefulness, and greed that we have legitimized here as economic virtues, and have taught to the world. They cannot protect us against our government's long-standing disdain for any form of self-sufficiency or thrift, or against the consequent dependence, which for the present at least is inescapable, on foreign supplies such as oil from the Middle East.

And they cannot protect us from what may prove to be the greatest danger of all: the estrangement of our people from one another and from our land. Increasingly, Americans—including, notoriously, their politicians—are not *from* anywhere. And so they have in this "homeland," which their government now seeks to make secure on their behalf, no home *place* that they are strongly moved to know or love or use well or protect.

It is no wonder that "The National Security Strategy," growing as it does out of unresolved contradictions in our domestic life, should attempt to compound a foreign policy out of contradictory principles.

There is, first of all, the contradiction of peace and war, or of war as the means of achieving and preserving peace. This document affirms peace; it also affirms peace as the justification of war and war as the means of peace—

and thus it perpetuates a hallowed absurdity. But implicit in its assertion of this (and, by implication, any other) nation's right to act alone in its own interest is an acceptance of war as a permanent condition. Either way, it is cynical to invoke the ideas of cooperation, community, peace, freedom, justice, dignity, and the rule of law (as this document repeatedly does), and then proceed to assert one's intention to act alone in making war. One cannot reduce terror by holding over the world the threat of what it most fears.

All the things we supposedly want to secure are thus subverted by our proposed means of securing them. Edmund Burke recognized this contradiction and was wary of it: "Laws are commanded to hold their tongues amongst arms; and tribunals fall to the ground with the peace they are no longer able to uphold."

This is a contradiction not reconcilable except by a self-righteousness almost inconceivably naive. The authors write that "We will . . . use our foreign aid to promote freedom and support those who struggle *non-violently* [my emphasis] for it"; and they observe that

> In pursuing advanced military capabilities that can threaten its neighbors
> . . . China is following an outdated path that, in the end, will hamper its
> own pursuit of national greatness. In time, China will find that social
> and political freedom is the only source of that greatness.

Thus we come to the authors' implicit definition of "rogue state": any nation pursuing national greatness by advanced military capabilities that can threaten its neighbors—any nation, that is, except *our* nation.

If you think our displeasure with "rogue states" might have any underpinning in international law, then you will be disappointed to learn that

> We will take the actions necessary to ensure that our efforts to meet our
> global security commitments and protect Americans are not impaired
> by the potential for investigations, inquiry, or prosecution by the Inter-
> national Criminal Court (ICC), whose jurisdiction does not extend to
> Americans and which we do not accept.

The rule of law in the world, then, is to be upheld by a nation that has declared itself to be above the law. A childish hypocrisy here assumes the dignity of a nation's foreign policy. But if we perceive an illegitimacy in the catastrophic weapons and *ad lib* warfare of other nations, how can we not perceive the same illegitimacy in our own?

The contradiction between peace and war implies, of course, at every point a contradiction between security and war. We wish, this document says, to be cooperative with other nations, but the authors seem not to realize how rigidly our diplomacy and our offers to cooperate will be qualified by this new threat of overwhelming force to be used merely at the president's pleasure. We cannot hope to be secure when our government has declared, by its announced readiness "to act alone," its willingness to be everybody's enemy.

III.

A further contradiction is that between war and commerce. This issue arises first of all in the war economy, which unsurprisingly regards war as a business and weapons as merchandise. However nationalistic may be the doctrine of "The National Security Strategy," the fact is that the business of warfare and the weapons trade have been thoroughly internationalized. Saddam Hussein possesses weapons of mass destruction, for example, partly because we sold him such weapons and the means of making them back when (madman or not) he was our "friend." But the internationalization of the weapons trade is a result inherent in international trade itself. It is a part of globalization. Mr. Bush's addition of this Security Strategy to the previous bipartisan commitment to globalization exposes an American dementia that has not been so plainly displayed before.

The America Whose Business Is Business has been internationalizing its economy in haste (for bad reasons, and with little foresight), looking everywhere for "trading partners," cheap labor, and tax shelters. Meanwhile, the America Whose Business Is National Defense is withdrawing from the world in haste (for bad reasons, with little foresight), threatening left and right, repudiating agreements, and angering friends. The problem of participating in the Global Economy for the benefit of Washington's corporate sponsors while maintaining a nationalist belligerence and an isolationist morality calls for superhuman intelligence in the Secretary of Commerce. The problem of "acting alone" in an international war while maintaining simultaneously our ability to import the foreign goods (for instance, oil) on which we have become dependent even militarily will call, likewise, for overtopping genius in the Secretary of Defense.

"The National Security Strategy" devotes a whole chapter to the president's resolve to "ignite a new era of global economic growth through free markets and free trade." But such a project cannot be wedded, even theoretically, to his commitment to a militarist nationalism ever prepared "to act alone." One must wonder when the government's corporate sponsors will see the contradiction and require the nation to assume a more humble posture in the presence of the global economy.

The conflict in future-abuse between this document and the sales talk of the corporations is stark, and it is pretty absurd. On the one hand, we have the future as a consumer's paradise in which everybody will be able to buy comfort, convenience, and happiness. On the other hand, we have this government's new future in which terrible things are bound to happen if we don't do terrible things in the present—which, of course, will make terrible things even more likely to happen in the future.

After World War II, we hoped the world might be united for the sake of peacemaking. Now the world is being "globalized" for the sake of trade and the so-called free market—for the sake, that is, of plundering the world for cheap labor, cheap energy, and cheap materials. How nations, let alone regions and communities, are to shape and protect themselves within this "global economy" is far from clear. Nor is it clear how the global economy can hope to survive the wars of nations.

If a nation cannot be "good" in any simple or incontestable way, then what can it reasonably be that is better than bad?

A nation can be charitable, as we can say with some confidence, for we need not look beyond our own for an example. Our nation, sometimes, has been charitable toward its own people; it has been kind to the elderly, the sick, the unemployed, and others unable to help themselves. And sometimes it has been charitable toward other nations, as when we helped even our onetime enemies to recover from World War II. But "charity" does not refer only to the institutional or governmental help we give to the "less fortunate." The word means "love." The commandment to "Love your enemies" suggests that charity must be without limit; it must include everything. A nation's charity must come from the heart and the imagination of its people. It requires us ultimately to see the world as a community of all the creatures, a community which, to be possessed by any, must be shared by all.

Perhaps that is only a better way of saying that a nation can be civilized. To be civil is to conduct oneself as a responsible citizen, honoring the lives and the rights of others. Our courts and jails are filled with the uncivil, who have presumed to act alone in their own interest. And we well know that incivility is now almost conventionally in business among us.

A nation can be independent, as our founders instructed us. If a nation cannot within reasonable measure be independent, it is hard to see how its existence might be justified. Though independence may at times require some sort of self-defense, it cannot be maintained by defiance of other nations or by making war against them. It can be maintained only by the most practical economic self-reliance. At the very least, a nation should be able sustainably to feed, clothe, and shelter its citizens, using its own sources and by its own work.

And of course that requires a nation to be, in the truest sense, patriotic: Its citizens must love their land with a knowing, intelligent, sustaining, and protective love. They must not, for any price, destroy its beauty, its health, or its productivity. And they must not allow their patriotism to be degraded to a mere loyalty to symbols or any present set of officials.

A nation also can abide under the rule of law. Since the Alien and Sedition Laws of 1798, in times of national stress or emergency there have been arguments for the abridgement of citizenship under the Constitution. But the weakness of those arguments is in their invariable implication that a democracy such as ours can work only in the most favorable circumstances. If constitutional guarantees of rights and immunities cannot be maintained in unfavorable circumstances, what is their point or value? Their value in fact originates in the acknowledgment of their usefulness in the times of greatest difficulty and to those in greatest need, as does the value of international law.

It is impossible to think that constitutional government can be suspended in a time of danger, in deference to the greater "efficiency" of centralized power, and then easily or quickly restored. Efficiency may be a political virtue, but only if strictly limited. Our Constitution, by its separation of powers and its system of checks and balances, acts as a restraint upon efficiency by denying exclusive power to any branch of the government. The logic of governmental efficiency, unchecked, runs straight on, not only to dictatorship, but also to torture, assassination, and other abominations.

Such aims as charity, civility, independence, true patriotism, and lawfulness a nation of imperfect human beings may reasonably adopt as its standards. And we may conclude reasonably, rightly, and with no touch of self-contempt, that by those standards we are less charitable, less civil, less independent, less patriotic, and less law-abiding than we might be, and than we need to be. And do these shortcomings relate to the president's perception that we are less secure than we need to be? We would be extremely foolish to suppose otherwise.

One might reasonably assume that a policy of national security would advocate from the start various practical measures to conserve and to use frugally the nation's resources, the objects of this husbandry being a reduction in the nation's dependence on imports and a reduction in the competition between nations for necessary goods. One might reasonably expect the virtues of stewardship, thrift, self-sufficiency, and neighborliness to receive a certain precedence in the advocacy of political leaders. Since the country, to make itself secure, may be required to rely on itself, one might reasonably expect a due concern for the health and longevity of its soils, forests, and watersheds, its natural and its human communities, its domestic economy, and the natural systems on which that economy inescapably depends.

Such a concern could come only from perceiving the contradiction between national security and the present global economy, but there is no such perception in "The National Security Strategy." This document, ignoring all conflicts, proposes to go straight ahead with both projects: national security, which it defines forthrightly as isolationist, domineering, and violent; and the global economy, which it defines as international humanitarianism. It does allow that there is a connection between our national security and the economic condition of "the rest of the world," and that the extreme poverty of much of the rest of the world is "neither just nor stable." And of course one can only agree. But the authors assume that economic wrongs can be righted merely by "economic development" and the "free market," that it is the nature of these things to cure poverty, and that they will not be impeded by terrorism or a war against terrorism or a preemptive war for the security of one nation. These are articles of a faith available only to a politically sheltered economic elite.

As for conservation here and elsewhere, the authors provide a list of proposals that is short, vague or ambiguous, incomplete, and rather wildly miscellaneous:

We will incorporate labor and environmental concerns into U.S. trade negotiations . . .

We will . . . expand the sources and types of global energy...

We will . . . develop cleaner and more energy efficient technologies.

Economic growth should be accompanied by global efforts to *stabilize* [my emphasis] greenhouse gas concentrations . . .

Our overall objective is to reduce America's greenhouse gas emissions relative to the size of our economy, cutting such emissions per unit of economic activity by 18 percent over the next 10 years . . .

But the only energy technologies specifically promoted here are those of "clean coal" and nuclear power—for both of which there is a strong corporate advocacy and a strong conservationist criticism or opposition. There is no mention of land loss, of soil erosion, of pollution of land, air, and water, or of the various threats to biological diversity—all problems of generally (and scientifically) recognized gravity.

Agriculture, which is involved with all the problems listed above, and with several others—and which is the economic activity most clearly and directly related to national security, if one grants that we all must eat—receives scant and superficial treatment amounting to dismissal. The document proposes only:

1. "a global effort to address new technology, science, and health regulations that needlessly impede farm exports and improved agriculture." This refers, without saying so, to the growing consumer resistance to genetically modified food. A global effort to overcome this resistance would help, not farmers and not consumers, but global agribusiness corporations such as Monsanto.

2. "transitional safeguards which we have used in the agricultural sector." This refers to government subsidies, which ultimately help the agribusiness corporations, not farmers.

3. Promotion of "new technologies, including biotechnology, [which] have enormous potential to improve crop yields in developing countries while using fewer pesticides and less water." This

is offered (as usual and questionably) as the solution to hunger, but its immediate benefit would be to the corporate suppliers of the technologies.

This is not an agriculture policy, let alone a national security strategy. It has the blindness, arrogance, and foolishness that are characteristic of top-down thinking by politicians and academic experts, assuming that "improved agriculture" would inevitably be the result of catering to the agribusiness corporations, and that national food security can be achieved merely by going on as before. It does not address any agricultural problem as such, and it ignores the vulnerability of our present food system—dependent as it is on genetically impoverished monocultures, cheap petroleum, cheap long-distance transportation, and cheap farm labor—to many kinds of disruption by "the embittered few," who, in the event of such disruption, would quickly become the embittered many. On eroding, ecologically degraded, increasingly toxic landscapes, worked by failing or subsidy-dependent farmers and by the cheap labor of migrants, we have erected the tottering tower of "agribusiness," which prospers and "feeds the world" (incompletely and temporarily) by undermining its own foundations.

But all our military strength, all our police, all our technologies and strategies of suspicion and surveillance cannot make us secure if we lose our ability to farm, or if we squander our forests, or if we exhaust or poison our water sources.

A policy of preemptive war that rests, as this one does, on such flimsy domestic underpinnings and on too great a concentration of power in the presidency, obviously risks or invites correction. And, as we know, correction can come by three means:

1. By strenuous public debate. But this requires a strong, independent political opposition, which at present we do not have. The country now contains many individuals and groups seriously troubled by issues of civil rights, food, health, agriculture, economy, peace, and conservation. These people have much in common, but they have no strong political voice, because few politicians have seen fit to speak for them.

2. By failure, as by some serious disruption of our food or transportation or energy systems. This might cause a principled and serious public debate, which might place us on a more stable economic and political footing. But we are a large nation, highly centralized in almost every way, and without much self-sufficiency, either national or regional. Any failure, therefore, will be large and not nearly so easy to correct as to prevent.

3. By citizens' initiative. Responsibilities abandoned by the government properly are assumed by the people. An example of this is the already well-established movement for local economies, typically beginning with food. There is much hope in this effort, provided that it continues to grow. And we have, surviving from the Vietnam War, a surprisingly strong and numerous peace movement. As we learned from the Vietnam experience, the only effective answer to a secretive and unresponsive government is a citizens' revolt. The revolt against the war in Vietnam was nonviolent, effective, and finally successful. Such a correction is better than no correction, but it is far from ideal—far less to be preferred than correction by public debate. A citizens' revolt necessarily comes too late. And if it is not peaceable and responsibly led, it could easily destroy the things it is meant to save.

IV.

The present administration has adopted a sort of official Christianity, and it obviously wishes to be regarded as Christian. But "Christian" war has always been a problem, best solved by avoiding any attempt to reconcile policies of national or imperial militarism with anything Christ said or did. The Christian gospel is a summons to peace, calling for justice beyond anger, mercy beyond justice, forgiveness beyond mercy, love beyond forgiveness. It would require a most agile interpreter to justify hatred and war by means of the Gospels, in which we are bidden to love our enemies, bless those who curse us, do good to those who hate us, and pray for those who despise and persecute us.

This peaceability has grown more practical—it has gained "survival value"—as industrial warfare has developed increasingly catastrophic weapons, which are abominable to our government, so far, only when other governments possess them. But since the end of World War II, when the terrors of industrial war had been fully revealed, many people and, by fits and starts, many governments have recognized that peace is not just a desirable condition, as was thought before, but is a practical necessity. It has become less and less thinkable that we might have a living and a livable world, or that we might have livable lives or any lives at all, if we do not make the world capable of peace.

And yet we have not learned to think of peace apart from war. We have received many teachings about peace and peaceability in biblical and other religious traditions, but we have marginalized those teachings, have made them abnormal, in deference to the great norm of violence and conflict. We wait, still, until we face terrifying dangers and the necessity to choose among bad alternatives, and then we think again of peace, and again we fight a war to secure it.

At the end of the war, if we have won it, we declare peace; we congratulate ourselves on our victory; we marvel at the newly proved efficiency of our latest, most "sophisticated" weapons; we ignore the cost in lives, materials, and property, in suffering and disease, in damage to the natural world; we ignore the inevitable residue of resentment and hatred; and we go on as before, having, as we think, successfully defended our way of life.

That is pretty much the story of our victory in the Gulf War of 1991. In the years between that victory and September 11, 2001, we did not alter our thinking about peace and war, which is to say that we thought much about war and little about peace; we continued to punish the defeated people of Iraq and their children; we made no effort to reduce our dependence on the oil we import from other, potentially belligerent countries; we made no improvement in our charity toward the rest of the world; we made no motion toward greater economic self-reliance; and we continued our extensive and often irreversible damages to our own land. We appear to have assumed merely that our victory confirmed our manifest destiny to be the richest, most powerful, most wasteful nation in the world. After the catastrophe of September 11, it again became clear to us how good it would be to be at peace, to have no enemies, to have no needless death to mourn. And then, our need for war following with the customary swift and deadly logic our need for peace, we took up the customary obsession with the evil of other people.

And now we are stirring up the question whether or not Islam is a war-like religion, ignoring the question, much more urgent for us, whether or not Christianity is a warlike religion. There is no hope in this. Islam, Judaism, Christianity—all have been warlike religions. All have tried to make peace and rid the world of evil by fighting wars. This has not worked. It is never going to work. The failure belongs inescapably to all of these religions inso-far as they have been warlike, and to acknowledge this failure is the duty of all of them. It is the duty of all of them to see that it is wrong to destroy the world, or risk destroying it, to get rid of its evil.

It is useless to try to adjudicate a long-standing animosity by asking who started it or who is the most wrong. The only sufficient answer is to give up the animosity and try forgiveness, to try to love our enemies and to talk to them and (if we pray) to pray for them. If we can't do any of that, then we must begin again by trying to imagine our enemies' children, who, like *our* children, are in mortal danger because of enmity that they did not cause.

We can no longer afford to confuse peaceability with passivity. Authen-tic peace is no more passive than war. Like war, it calls for discipline and intelligence and strength of character, though it calls also for higher prin-ciples and aims. If we are serious about peace, then we must work for it as ardently, seriously, continuously, carefully, and bravely as we have ever pre-pared for war.

(2003)

Thoughts in the Presence of Fear

I. The time will soon come when we will not be able to remember the horrors of September 11 without remembering also the unquestioning technological and economic optimism that ended on that day.

II. This optimism rested on the proposition that we were living in a "new world order" and a "new economy" that would "grow" on and on, bringing a prosperity of which every new increment would be "unprecedented."

III. The dominant politicians, corporate officers, and investors who believed this proposition did not acknowledge that the prosperity was limited to a tiny percentage of the world's people, and to an ever smaller number of people even in the United States; that it was founded upon the oppressive labor of poor people all over the world; and that its ecological costs increasingly threatened all life, including the lives of the supposedly prosperous.

IV. The "developed" nations had given to the "free market" the status of a religion, and were sacrificing to it their farmers, farmlands, and rural communities, their forests, wetlands, and prairies, their ecosystems and watersheds. They had accepted universal pollution and global warming as normal costs of doing business.

V. There was, as a consequence, a growing worldwide effort on behalf of economic decentralization, economic justice, and ecological responsibility. We must recognize that the events of September 11 make this effort more necessary than ever. We citizens of the industrial countries must continue the labor of self-criticism and self-correction. We must recognize our mistakes.

VI. The paramount doctrine of the economic and technological euphoria of recent decades has been that everything depends on innovation. It was understood as desirable, and even as necessary, that we should go on and on from one technological innovation to the next, which would cause the economy to "grow" and make everything better and better. This of course implied at every point a hatred of the past, of all things inherited and free. All things superseded in our progress of innovations, whatever their value might have been, were discounted as of no value at all.

VII. We did not anticipate anything like what has now happened. We did not foresee that all our sequence of innovations might be at once over-ridden by a greater one: the invention of a new kind of war that would turn our previous innovations against us, discovering and exploiting the debits and the dangers that we had ignored. We never considered the possibility that we might be trapped in the webwork of communication and transport that was supposed to make us free.

VIII. Nor did we foresee that the weaponry and the war science that we marketed and taught to the world would become available, not just to recognized national governments which possess so uncannily the power to legitimate large-scale violence, but also to "rogue nations," dissident or fanatical groups, and individuals—whose violence, though never worse than that of nations, is judged by the nations to be illegitimate.

IX. We had apparently accepted the belief that technology is only good; that it cannot serve evil as well as good; that it cannot serve our enemies as well as ourselves; that it cannot be used to destroy what is good, including our homelands and our lives.

X. We had accepted too the corollary belief that an economy (either as a money economy or as a life-support system) that is global in extent, technologically complex, and centralized is invulnerable to terrorism, sabotage, or war, and that it is protectable by "national defense."

XI. We now have a clear, inescapable choice that we must make. We can continue to promote a global economic system of unlimited "free trade" among corporations, held together by long and highly vulnerable lines of communication and supply, but *now* recognizing that such a system will have to be protected by a hugely expensive police force that will be worldwide, whether maintained by one nation or several or all, and that such a police force will be effective precisely to the extent that it over-sways the freedom and privacy of the citizens of every nation.

XII. Or we can promote a decentralized world economy that would have the aim of assuring to every nation and region a *local* self-sufficiency in life-supporting goods. This would not eliminate international trade, but it would tend toward a trade in surpluses after local needs have been met.

XIII. One of the gravest dangers to us now, second only to further terror-ist attacks against our people, is that we will attempt to go on as before with the corporate program of global "free trade," whatever the cost in freedom and civil rights, without self-questioning or self-criticism or public debate.

XIV. This is why the substitution of rhetoric for thought, always a temp-tation in a national crisis, must be resisted by officials and citizens alike. It is hard for ordinary citizens to know what is actually happening in Washington in a time of such great trouble; for all we know, serious and difficult thought may be taking place there. But the talk that we are hearing from politicians, bureaucrats, and commentators has so far tended to reduce the complex problems now facing us to issues of unity, security, normality, and retaliation.

XV. National self-righteousness, like personal self-righteousness, is a mis-take. It is misleading. It is a sign of weakness. Any war that we may make now against terrorism will come as a new installment in a history of war in which we have fully participated. We are not innocent of making war against civilian populations. The modern doctrine of such warfare was set forth and enacted by General William Tecumseh Sherman, who held that a civilian population could be declared guilty and rightly subjected to military punishment. We have never repudiated that doctrine.

XVI. It is a mistake also—as events since September 11 have shown—to suppose that a government can promote and participate in a global economy and at the same time act exclusively in its own interest by abrogating its international treaties and standing aloof from international cooperation on moral issues.

XVII. And surely, in our country, under our Constitution, it is a fundamental error to suppose that any crisis or emergency can justify any form of political oppression. Since September 11, far too many public voices have presumed to "speak for us" in saying that Americans will gladly accept a reduction of freedom in exchange for greater "security." Some would, maybe. But some others would accept a reduction in security (and in global trade) far more willingly than they would accept any abridgement of our constitutional rights.

XVIII. In a time such as this, when we have been seriously and most cruelly hurt by those who hate us, and when we must consider ourselves to be gravely threatened by those same people, it is hard to speak of the ways of peace and to remember that Christ enjoined us to love our enemies, but this is no less necessary for being difficult.

XIX. Even now we dare not forget that since the attack on Pearl Harbor— to which the present attack has been often and not usefully compared— we humans have suffered an almost uninterrupted sequence of wars, none of which have brought peace or made us more peaceable.

XX. The aim and result of war necessarily are not peace but victory, and any victory won by violence necessarily justifies the violence that won it and leads to further violence. If we are serious about innovation, must we not conclude that we need something new to replace our perpetual "war to end war"?

XXI. What leads to peace is not violence but peaceableness, which is not passivity, but an alert, informed, practiced, and active state of being. We should recognize that while we have extravagantly subsidized the means of war, we have almost totally neglected the ways of peaceableness. We have, for example, several national military academies, but not one peace academy. We have ignored the teachings and the examples of Christ, Gandhi, Martin Luther King, and other peaceable leaders. And here we have an inescapable duty to notice also that war is profitable, whereas the means of peaceableness, being cheap or free, make no money.

XXII. The key to peaceableness is continuous practice. It is wrong to suppose that we can exploit and impoverish the poorer countries, while arming them and instructing them in the newest means of war, and then reasonably expect them to be peaceable.

XXIII. We must not again allow public emotion or the public media to caricature our enemies. If our enemies are now to be some nations of Islam, then we should undertake to *know* those enemies. Our schools should begin to teach the histories, cultures, arts, and languages of the Islamic nations. And our leaders should have the humility and the wisdom to ask the reasons some of those people have for hating us.

XXIV. Starting with the economies of food and farming, we should promote at home and encourage abroad the ideal of local self-sufficiency. We should recognize that this is the surest, the safest, and the cheapest way for the world to live. We should not countenance the loss or destruction of any local capacity to produce necessary goods.

XXV. We should reconsider and renew and extend our efforts to protect the natural foundations of the human economy: soil, water, and air. We should protect every intact ecosystem and watershed that we have left, and begin restoration of those that have been damaged.

XXVI. The complexity of our present trouble suggests as never before that we need to change our present concept of education. Education is not properly an industry, and its proper use is not to serve industries, either by job-training or by industry-subsidized research. Its proper use is to enable citizens to live lives that are economically, politically, socially, and culturally responsible. This cannot be done by gathering or "accessing" what we now call "information"—which is to say facts without context and therefore without priority. A proper education enables young people to put their lives in order, which means knowing what things are more important than other things; it means putting first things first.

XXVII. The first thing we must begin to teach our children (and learn ourselves) is that we cannot spend and consume endlessly. We have got to learn to save and conserve. We do need a "new economy," but one that is founded on thrift and care, on saving and conserving, not on excess and waste. An economy based on waste is inherently and hopelessly violent, and war is its inevitable by-product. We need a peaceable economy.

(2001)

The Failure of War

IF YOU KNOW even as little history as I know, it is hard not to doubt the efficacy of modern war as a solution to any problem except that of retribution—the "justice" of exchanging one damage for another, which results only in doubling (and continuing) the damage and the suffering.

Apologists for war will immediately insist that war answers the problem of national self-defense. But the doubter, in reply, will ask to what extent the *cost* even of a successful war of national defense—in life, money, material goods, health, and (inevitably) freedom—may amount to a national defeat. And national defense in war always involves *some* degree of national defeat. This paradox has been with us from the very beginning of our republic. Militarization in defense of freedom reduces the freedom of the defenders. There is a fundamental inconsistency between war and freedom.

In asking such a question, the doubter will be mindful also that in a modern war, fought with modern weapons and on the modern scale, neither side can limit to "the enemy" or "the enemy country" the damage that it does. These wars damage the world. We know enough by now to know that you cannot damage a part of the world without damaging all of it. Modern war has not only made it impossible to kill "combatants" without killing "noncombatants," it has made it impossible to damage your enemy without damaging yourself. You cannot kill your enemy's women and children without offering your own women and children to the selfsame possibility. We (and, inevitably, others) have prepared ourselves to destroy our enemy by destroying the entire world—including, of course, ourselves.

That many have considered the increasing unacceptability of modern warfare is shown by the language of the propaganda surrounding modern war. Modern wars have characteristically been fought to end war. They have been fought in the name of peace. Our most terrible weapons have been made, ostensibly, to preserve and assure the peace of the world. "All we want is peace," we say, as we increase relentlessly our capacity to make war.

And yet at the end of a century in which we have fought two wars to end war and several more to prevent war and preserve peace, and in which scientific and technological progress has made war ever more terrible and less controllable in its effects, we still, by policy, give no consideration, and no countenance, to nonviolent means of national defense. We do indeed make much of diplomacy and diplomatic relations, but by diplomacy we mean invariably ultimatums for peace backed by the threat of war. It is always understood that we stand ready to kill those with whom we are "peacefully negotiating."

Our century of war, militarism, and political terror has unsurprisingly produced great—and successful!—advocates of true peace, among whom Mohandas K. Gandhi and Martin Luther King, Jr., are paramount examples. The considerable success that they achieved testifies to the presence, in the midst of violence, of an authentic and powerful desire for peace and, more important, of the proven will to make the necessary sacrifices. But so far as our government is concerned, these men and their great and authenticating accomplishments might as well never have existed. To achieve peace by peaceable means is not yet our goal. We cling to the hopeless paradox of making peace by making war.

Which is to say that we cling, in our public life, to a brutal hypocrisy. In our century of almost universal violence of humans against fellow humans and against our natural and cultural commonwealth, hypocrisy has been inescapable because our opposition to violence has been selective or merely fashionable. Some of us who approve of our monstrous military budget and our peacekeeping wars nonetheless deplore "domestic violence" and think that our society can be pacified by "gun control." Some of us are against capital punishment but for abortion. Some of us are against abortion but for capital punishment. Most of us, whatever our stand on preserving the lives of the thoughtlessly conceived unborn, thoughtlessly participate in an economy that steals from all the unborn.

One does not have to know very much or think very far in order to see the moral absurdity upon which we have erected our sanctioned enterprises of violence. Abortion-as-birth-control is justified as a "right," which can establish itself only by denying all the rights of another person, which is the most primitive intent of warfare. Capital punishment sinks us all to the same level of primal belligerence, at which an act of violence is avenged by another act of violence. What the justifiers of these wrongs ignore is the fact—as well established by the history of feuds or the history of anger as by the history of war—that violence breeds violence. Acts of violence committed in "justice" or in affirmation of "rights" or in defense of "peace" do not end violence. They prepare and justify its continuation.

The most dangerous superstition of the parties of violence is the idea that sanctioned violence can prevent or control unsanctioned violence. But if violence is "just" in one instance, as determined by the state, why, by a merely logical extension, might it not also be "just" in another instance, as determined by an individual? How can a society that justifies capital punishment and warfare prevent its justifications from being extended to assassination and terrorism? If a government perceives that some causes are so important as to justify the killing of children, how can it hope to prevent the contagion of its logic from spreading to its citizens—or to its citizens' children? If you so devalue human life that the accidentally conceived unborn may be permissibly killed, how do you keep that permission from being assumed by someone who has made the same judgment against the born?

I am aware of the difficulty of assigning psychological causes to acts of violence. Psychological causes abound. But here I am talking about the power of example, precedent, and reason.

If we give to these small absurdities the magnitude of international relations, we produce, unsurprisingly, some much larger absurdities. What could be more absurd than our attitude of high moral outrage against other nations for manufacturing the selfsame weapons that we manufacture? The difference, as our leaders say, is that we will use these weapons virtuously whereas our enemies will use them maliciously—a proposition that too readily conforms to a proposition of much less dignity: We will use them in *our* interest, whereas our enemies will use them in *theirs*. The issue of virtue in war is as obscure, ambiguous, and troubling as Abraham Lincoln found to be the issue of prayer in war: "Both [the North and the South] read the same Bible, and pray to the same God; and each invokes His aid against the other. . . . The prayers of both could not be answered—that of neither could be answered fully."

But recent American wars, having been both "foreign" and "limited," have been fought under a second illusion even more dangerous than the illusion of perfect virtue: We are assuming, and are encouraged by our leaders to assume, that, aside from the sacrifice of life, no personal sacrifice is required. In "foreign" wars, we do not directly experience the damage that we inflict upon the enemy. We hear and see this damage reported in the news, but we are not affected, and we don't mind. These limited, "foreign" wars require that some of our young people will be killed or crippled, and that some families will grieve, but these "casualties" are so widely distributed among our population as hardly to be noticed. Otherwise, we do not feel ourselves to be involved. We pay taxes to support the war, but that is nothing new, for we pay war taxes also in time of "peace." We experience no shortages, we suffer no rationing, we endure no limitations. We earn, borrow, spend, and consume in wartime as in peacetime.

And of course no sacrifice is required of those large economic interests that now principally constitute our "economy." No corporation will be required to submit to any limitation or to sacrifice a dollar. On the contrary, war is understood by some as the great cure-all and opportunity of our corporate economy. War ended the Great Depression of the 1930's, and we have maintained a war economy—an economy, one might justly say, of general violence—ever since, sacrificing to it an enormous economic and ecological wealth, including, as designated victims, the farmers and the industrial working class.

And so great costs are involved in our fixation on war, but the costs are "externalized" as "acceptable losses." And here we see how progress in war, progress in technology, and progress in the industrial economy are parallel to one another—or, very often, are merely identical.

Romantic nationalists, which is to say most apologists for war, always imply in their public speeches a mathematics or an accounting that cannot be performed. Thus by its suffering in the Civil War, the North is said to have "paid for" the emancipation of the slaves and the preservation of the Union. Thus we may speak of our liberty as having been "bought" by the bloodshed of patriots. I am fully aware of the truth in such statements. I know that I am one of many who have benefited from painful sacrifices made by other people, and I would not like to be ungrateful. Moreover, I am a patriot myself, and I know that the time may come for any of us when we must make extreme sacrifices for the sake of liberty.

But still I am suspicious of this kind of accounting. For one reason, it is necessarily done by the living on behalf of the dead. And I think we must be careful about too easily accepting, or being too easily grateful for, sacrifices made by others, especially if we have made none ourselves. For another reason, though our leaders in war always assume that there is an acceptable price, there is never a previously stated level of acceptability. The acceptable price, finally, is whatever is paid.

It is easy to see the similarity between this accounting of the price of war and our usual accounting of "the price of progress." We seem to have agreed that whatever has been (or will be) paid for so-called progress is an acceptable price. If that price includes the diminishment of privacy and the increase of government secrecy, so be it. If it means a radical reduction in the number of small businesses and the virtual destruction of the farm population, so be it. If it means cultural and ecological impoverishment, so be it. If it means the devastation of whole regions by extractive industries, so be it. If it means that a mere handful of people should own more billions of wealth than is owned by all of the world's poor, so be it.

But let us have the candor to acknowledge that what we call "the economy" or "the free market" is less and less distinguishable from warfare. For about half of this century we worried about world conquest by international communism. Now with less worry (so far) we are witnessing world conquest by international capitalism. Though its political means are milder (so far) than those of communism, this newly internationalized capitalism may prove even more destructive of human cultures and communities, of freedom, and of nature. Its tendency is just as much toward total dominance and control. Confronting this conquest, ratified and licensed by the new international trade agreements, no place and no community in the world may consider itself safe from some form of plunder. More and more people all over the world are recognizing that this is so, and they are saying that world conquest of any kind is wrong, period.

They are doing more than that. They are saying that *local* conquest also is wrong, and wherever it is taking place local people are joining together to oppose it. All over my own state of Kentucky this opposition is growing— from the west, where the exiled people of the Land Between the Lakes are struggling to save their confiscated homeland from bureaucratic degradation, to the east, where the native people of the mountains are still struggling to preserve their land from destruction by absentee corporations.

To have an economy that is warlike, that aims at conquest, and that destroys virtually everything that it is dependent on, placing no value on the health of nature or of human communities, is absurd enough. It is even more absurd that this economy, that in some respects is so much at one with our military industries and programs, is in other respects directly in conflict with our professed aim of national defense.

It seems only reasonable, only sane, to suppose that a gigantic program of preparedness for national defense would be founded, first of all, upon a principle of national and even regional economic independence. A nation determined to defend itself and its freedoms should be prepared, and always preparing, to live from its own resources and from the work and the skills of its own people. It should carefully husband and conserve those resources, justly compensate that work, and rigorously cultivate and nurture those skills. But that is not what we are doing in the United States today. What we are doing, as we prepare for and prosecute wars allegedly for national defense, is squandering in the most prodigal manner the natural and human resources of the nation.

At present, in the face of declining finite sources of fossil fuel energy, we have virtually no energy policy, either for conservation or for the development of safe and clean alternative sources. At present, our energy policy simply is to use all that we have. At present, moreover, in the face of a growing population needing to be fed, we have virtually no policy for land conservation, and *no* policy of just compensation to the primary producers of food. At present, our agricultural policy is to use up everything that we have, while depending increasingly on imported food, energy, technology, and labor.

Those are just two examples of our general indifference to our own needs. We thus are elaborating a direct and surely a dangerous contradiction between our militant nationalism and our espousal of the international "free market" ideology. How are we going to defend our freedoms (this is a question both for militarists and for pacifists) when we must import our necessities from international suppliers who have no concern or respect for our freedoms? What would happen if in the course of a war of national defense we were to be cut off from our foreign sources of supply? What would happen if, in a war of national defense, military necessity required us to attack or blockade our foreign suppliers? We have already fought one energy war allegedly in national defense. If our present policies of economic indifference continue, we may face wars for other commodities: food or water or shoes or steel or textiles.

What can we do to free ourselves of this absurdity?

With that question my difficulty declares itself, for I do not ask it as a teacher knowing the answer. I ask it knowing that by doing so I describe my own dilemma. The news media, the industrial economy, perhaps human nature as well, prompt us to want quick, neat answers to our questions, but I don't think my question has a quick, neat answer.

Obviously, we would be less absurd if we took better care of one another and of all our fellow creatures. We would be less absurd if we founded our public policies upon an honest description of our needs and our predicament, rather than upon fantastical descriptions of our wishes. We would be less absurd if our leaders would consider in good faith the proven alternatives to violence.

Such things are easy to say. But finally we must face this daunting question, not as a nation or a group, but as individual persons—as ourselves. We are disposed, somewhat by culture and somewhat by nature, to solve our problems by violence—by maximum force relentlessly applied—and even to enjoy doing so. And yet by now all of us must at least have suspected that our right to live, to be free, and to be at peace is not guaranteed by any act of violence. It can be guaranteed only by our willingness that all other persons should live, be free, and be at peace—and by our willingness to use or give our own lives to make that possible. To be incapable of such willingness is merely to resign ourselves to the absurdity we are in; and yet, if you are like me, you are unsure to what extent you are capable of it.

It appears then that the answer to my question may be only another question. But maybe we can take some encouragement from that. Maybe, if our questions lead to other questions, that is a sign that we are asking the right ones.

Here is the other question that the predicament of modern warfare forces upon us: How many deaths of other people's children by bombing or starvation are we willing to accept in order that we may be free, affluent, and (supposedly) at peace? To that question I answer pretty quickly: *None*. And I know that I am not the only one who would give that answer: Please. No children. Don't kill any children for *my* benefit.

If that is our answer, then we must know that we have not come to rest. Far from it. For now surely we must feel ourselves swarmed about with more questions that are urgent, personal, and intimidating. But perhaps also we feel ourselves beginning to be free, facing at last in our own lives the greatest challenge ever laid before us, the most comprehensive vision of human progress, the best advice and the least obeyed:

"Love your enemies, bless them that curse you, do good to them that hate you, and pray for them which despitefully use you, and persecute you;

"That ye may be the children of your Father which is in Heaven: for He maketh His sun to rise on the evil and the good, and sendeth rain on the just and on the unjust."

(1999)

Postscript

I have been advised that "most readers" will object to my treatment of abortion in this essay. I don't know that most readers will object, but I am sure that some will. And so I will deal with this subject more plainly.

The issue of abortion, so far as I understand it, involves two questions: Is it killing? And what is killed?

It is killing, of course. To kill is the express purpose of the procedure.

What is killed is usually described by apologists for abortion as "a fetus," as if that term names a distinct kind or species of being. But what this being might be, if it is not a human being, is not clear. Generally, pregnant women have thought and spoken of the beings in their wombs as "babies." The attempt to make a categorical distinction between a baby living in the womb and a baby living in the world is as tenuous as would be an attempt to make such a distinction between a living child and a living adult. No living creature is "viable" independently of an enveloping life-support system.

If the creature in the womb is a living human being, and so far also an innocent one, then it is wrong to treat it as an enemy. If we are worried about the effects of treating fellow humans as enemies or enemies of society eligible to be killed, how do we justify treating an innocent fellow human as an enemy-in-the-womb?

As for the "right to control one's own body," I am all for that. But implicit in that right is the responsibility to control one's body in such a way as to avoid dealing irresponsibly or violently or murderously with other bodies.

Women and men generally have understood that when they have conceived a child they have relinquished a significant measure of their independence, and that henceforth they must control their bodies in the interest
of the child.

(2003)

Going to Work

———————————— ⁓ ————————————

I. To live, we must go to work.

II. To work, we must work in a place.

III. Work affects everything in the place where it is done: the nature of the place itself and what is naturally there, the local ecosystem and watershed, the local landscape and its productivity, the local human neighborhood, the local memory.

IV. Much modern work is done in academic or professional or industrial or electronic enclosures. The work is thus enclosed in order to achieve a space of separation between the workers and the effects of their work. The enclosure permits the workers to think that they are working nowhere or anywhere—in their careers or specialties, perhaps, or in "cyberspace."

V. Nevertheless, their work will have a precise and practical influence, first on the place where it is being done, and then on every place where its products are used, on every place where its attitude toward its products is felt, on every place to which its by-products are carried.

VI. There is, in short, no way to escape the problems of effect and influence.

VII. The responsibility of the worker is to confront these problems and deal justly with them. How is this possible?

VIII. It is possible only if the worker knows and accepts the reality of the context of the work. The problems of effect and influence are inescapable because, whether acknowledged or not, work always has a context. Work must "take place." It takes place in a neighborhood and in a commonwealth.

IX. What, therefore, must we have in mind when we go to work? If we go to work with the aim of working well, we must have a lot in mind. What must we know? We can establish the curriculum by a series of questions:

X. *Who are we?* That is, who are we as we approach the work in its inevitable place? Where are we from, and what did we learn there, and (if we have left) why did we leave? What have we learned, starting perhaps with the influences that surrounded us before birth? What have we learned in school? More important, what have we learned *out* of school? What knowledge have we mastered? What skills? What tools? What affections, loyalties, and allegiances have we formed? What do we bring to the work?

XI. *Where are we?* What is this place in which we are preparing to do our work? What has happened here in geologic time? What has happened here in human time? What is the nature, what is the *genius,* of this place? What, if we weren't here, would nature be doing here? What will the nature of the place permit us to do here without exhausting either the place itself or the birthright of those who will come later? What, even, might nature help us to do here? Under what conditions, imposed both by the genius of the place and the genius of our arts, might our work here be healthful and beautiful?

XII. What do we have, in this place and in ourselves, that is good? What do we need? What do we want? How much of the good that is here, that we now have, are we willing to give up in the effort to have further goods that we need, that we think we need, or that we want?

XIII. And so our curriculum of questions, revealing what we have in mind, brings us to the crisis of the modern world. Partly this crisis is a confusion between needs and wants. Partly it is a crisis of rationality.

XIV. The confusion between needs and wants is, of course, fundamental. And let us make no mistake here: This is an *educated* confusion. Modern education systems have pretty consciously encouraged young people to think of their wants as needs. And the schools have increasingly advertised education as a way of getting what one wants; so that now, by a fairly logical progression, schools are understood by politicians and school bureaucrats merely as servants of "the economy." And by "the economy" they do not mean local households, livelihoods, and landscapes; they mean the corporate economy.

XV. But the idea that schools can have everything to do with the corporate economy and nothing to do with the health of their local watersheds and ecosystems and communities is a falsehood that has now run its course. It is a falsehood and nothing else.

XVI. What actually *do* we need? We might say that, at a minimum, we need food, clothing, and shelter. And, if we are wise, we might hasten to add that we don't want to live a minimal life; we would also count comfort, pleasure, health, and beauty as necessities. And then, with the realization that it may be possible by reducing our needs to reduce our humanity, we may want to say also that we will need to remember our history; we will need to preserve teachings and artifacts from the past; we will need leisure to study and contemplate these things; we will need towns or cities, places of economic and cultural exchange; we will need clean air to breathe, clean water to drink, wholesome food to eat, a healthful countryside, places in which we can know the natural world— and so on.

XVII. Well, now we see that in attempting to solve our problem we have run back into it. We have seen that in order to understand ourselves as fully human we have to define our necessities pretty broadly. How do we know when we have passed from needs to wants, from necessity to frivolity?

XVIII. That is an extremely difficult and troubling question, which is why it is also an extremely interesting question and one that we should not cease to ask. I can't answer it fully or confidently, but will only say in passing that our great modern error is the belief that we must invariably give up one thing in order to have another. But it is possible, for instance, to find comfort, pleasure, and beauty in food, clothing, and shelter. It is possible to find pleasure and beauty and even "recreation" in work. It is possible to have farms that do not waste and poison the natural world. It is possible to have productive forests that are not treated as "crops." It is possible to have cities that are ecologically, economically, socially, culturally, and architecturally continuous with their landscapes. It is not invariably necessary to *travel* from a need to its satisfaction, or from one satisfaction to another.

XIX. It is not invariably necessary to give up one good thing in order to have another. In our age of the world there is a kind of mind that is trying to be totally rational, which is in effect to say totally economic. This mind is now dominant. It is always telling us that the good things we have are really not as good as they seem, that they can seem good only to "backward people," and they certainly are not as good as the things we will have in the future, if only we will give up the things that seem good to us now. If a forest or a farm is destroyed to make a "housing development," and the "housing development" is then sacrificed to a factory or an airport, the rational mind wants us to believe that this course of changes is "progress," and it offers as proof the successive increases in the value or the profitability of the land. It shows us the "cost-benefit ratio." And here we arrive at the crisis of rationality. We have come to the point at which reason fails.

XX. Reason fails precisely in the inability of the cost-benefit ratio to include all the costs. We know that, however favorable may be the cost-benefit ratio, the progress from forest or farm to any sort of "development" degrades or destroys the integrity of the local ecosystem and watershed, and we know that it causes human heartbreak. This kind of accounting excludes all coherences except its own, and it excludes affection. The cost-benefit ratio is limited to what is handily quantifiable, namely money. The failure of reason comes to light in the recognition that things which cannot be quantified—the health of watersheds, the integrity of ecosystems, the wholeness of human hearts—ultimately affect the durability, availability, and affordability of necessary quantities.

To think of landscapes merely in terms of economic value will in the long run reduce their economic value, not to mention the availability of such necessities as timber and food, clean water and clean air.

XXI. The mind makes itself totally rational in an effort to become totally comfortable, but at the risk of eventually becoming totally uncomfortable. The cost of subordinating all value to economic value will eventually be economic failure.

XXII. We are well-acquainted with this mind of would-be total rationality, hell-bent on quantification. And we are increasingly well-acquainted with its results in the ruin of culture and nature. And so the next in our curriculum of questions necessarily is this: Do we know of a different or better or saner kind of mind?

XXIII. I think we do. It is what I would call the affectionate or sympathetic mind. This mind is not irrational, but neither is it primarily rational. It is a mind less comfortable than the mind that aspires only to reason, and it is more difficult to define.

XXIV. It is defined, I think, in the parable of the lost sheep in the Gospels of Matthew and Luke, and in the Buddhist vow: "Sentient beings are numberless, I vow to save them." The mind given over to reason would lose no time in demonstrating mathematically that it "makes no sense" to leave ninety-nine sheep perhaps in danger while you go to look for only one that is lost. And surely it makes even less "sense" to vow to "save" all sentient beings.

XXV. Obviously, to assent to such teachings as these we must change our minds. We must give up some part of our allegiance to reason and to quantification, and we must accept as our lot in life a perhaps irreducible discomfort. We have given affection and sympathy a priority over rationality. We have consented to the proposition that at least a part of what we have now, the part we have been given, is good, and we have assumed the responsibility of preserving the good that we have. We have assented implicitly to God's approval of His work on Creation's seventh day.

XXVI. To change one's mind in this way is to change the way one works. This changed way of working is new to us in our industrial age, but is old in the history of human making. And what is this way? How does this changed mind go about its work?

XXVII. Such a mind, I think, is no longer satisfied with the conventional standards of industrialism: profitability and utility. Needing a more authentic, more comprehensive criterion, it looks beyond those concerns, without necessarily giving them up. It tries to see the work and the product in context; it tries to derive its standards from that context. And once again it must proceed by way of questions: Is the worker diminished or in any other way abused by this work? What is the effect of the work upon the place, its ecosystem, its watershed, its atmosphere, its community? What is the effect of the product upon its user, and upon the place where it is used?

XXVIII. Work under the discipline of such questions might hope to give us, to name a few examples, forestry that would not destroy the forest, farming that would not destroy the land, houses that would be suited to their places in the landscape, products of all kinds that would neither exhaust their sources nor degrade their users.

XXIX. Obviously, there has come to be a radical disconnection between the arts and sciences and their ultimate context, which is always the natural or the given world. Why should this be?

XXX. I venture to think that it is a problem of perception, most particularly and directly in the sciences. The scientific need for predictability or replicability forces perception into abstraction. The "test plot," for example, is perceived, not as itself, but as a plot *representative* of all plots everywhere.

XXXI. Developers of technology, in somewhat the same way, are under commercial pressure for *general* applicability. The place where a new machine or chemical or technique is proved workable is assumed to be *representative* of all places where it might work.

XXXII. These processes in science and technology seem to be closely parallel in effect to the processes of centralization in economic and political power.

XXXIII. The result is that all landscapes, and the people and other creatures in them, are being manipulated for profit by people who can neither see them in their particularity nor care particularly about them.

XXXIV. The disciplines that are not directly involved in this manipulation nonetheless have consented to it. It is the problem of *all* the disciplines.

XXXV. It seems to me that the solution to this problem is not now foreseeable, but I believe it can come about only by widening the context of all intellectual work and of teaching—perhaps to the width of the local landscape.

XXXVI. To accept so wide a context, the disciplines would have to move away from strict or exclusive professionalism. This does not imply giving up professional competence or professional standards, which have their place, but professionalism as we now understand it has already shown itself to be inadequate to a wide context. To bring local landscapes within what Wes Jackson calls "the boundary of consideration," professional people of all sorts will have to feel the emotions and take the risks of amateurism. They will have to get out of their fields, so to speak, and into the watershed, the ecosystem, and the community; and they will have to be actuated by affection.

XXXVII. In the sciences, I think the acceptance of the local landscape as context will end the era of scientific heroism. No one scientist or one team of scientists or one science-exploiting corporation can expect to "save the world," once the disciplines have accepted this context that is at once wide and local. The solutions then will have to be local, and there will have to be a myriad of them. The scientists, moreover, will have to suffer the responsibility of applying their knowledge at home, sharing the fate of the place where their knowledge is applied.

XXXVIII. Throughout these notes I have been assuming—as my reading and the work I have done have taught me to assume—that it is impossible for us humans to know in any complete or final way what we are doing.

XXXIX. Now I will explain this assumption in a different way, but one that leads to the same conclusion.

XL. Increasingly since the Renaissance, the building blocks of rational thought have been facts, pieces of data that can be proved or demonstrated or observed to be "true."

XLI. The assumption seems to be that the pursuit of truth in our time, as never in the times before, has become completely scientific and rational, so that now we not only possess more facts every day than we ever possessed before, but have only to continue to fill in the gaps between facts by the empirical processes of our science until we will know the ultimate and entire truth.

XLII. I do not believe this. I think it is a kind of folly to assume that new knowledge is necessarily truer than old knowledge, or that empirical truth is truer than nonempirical truth. But I also do not believe that factual truth is or ever can be sufficient truth, let alone ultimate truth.

XLIII. A fact, I assume, is not a thing, but is something known about a thing. The formula H_2O is a fact about water; it is not water. A person who had never seen water could not recognize it, much less recognize ice or steam, from knowing the formula. Recognition would require knowledge of many more facts. Water is water because it is the absolute sum of all the facts about itself, and it would be itself whether or not humans knew all the facts.

XLIV. The only true representation of a thing, we can say, is the thing itself. This is true also of a person. It is true of a place. It is true of the world and all its creatures. The only true picture of Reality is Reality itself.

XLV. In order to work, in order to live, we humans necessarily make what we might call pictures of our world, of our places, of ourselves and one another. But these pictures are artifacts, human-made. And we can make them only by selection, choosing some things to put in the picture, and leaving out all the rest.

XLVI. From the standpoint of the person, place, or thing itself, of Reality itself, it doesn't make any difference whether our pictures are factual or imagined, made by science or by art or by both. All of them literally are fictions—things made by humans, things never equal to the reality they are about and never assuredly even adequate to the reality they are about.

XLVII. Facts in isolation are false. The more isolated a fact or a set of facts is, the more false it is. A fact is true in the absolute sense only in association with *all* facts. This is why the departmentalization of knowledge in our colleges and universities is fundamentally wrong.

XLVIII. Because our pictures of realities, and of Reality, are necessarily incomplete, they are always to some degree false and misleading. If they become too selective, if they exclude too much (on the ground, for instance, of being "not factual"), if they are too biased, they become dangerous. They are constantly subject to correction—by new facts, of course, but also by experience, by intuition, and by faith.

XLIX. We may say, then, that our sciences and arts owe a certain courtesy to Reality, and that this courtesy can be enacted only by humility, reverence, propriety of scale, and good workmanship.

(2000)

In Distrust of Movements

———— ✦ ————

I MUST BURDEN MY READERS as I have burdened myself with the knowledge that I speak from a local, some might say a provincial, point of view. When I try to identify myself to myself I realize that, in my most immediate reasons and affections, I am less than an American, less than a Kentuckian, less even than a Henry Countian, but am a man most involved with and concerned about my family, my neighbors, and the land that is daily under my feet. It is this involvement that defines my citizenship in the larger entities. And so I will remember, and I ask you to remember, that I am not trying to say what is thinkable everywhere, but rather what it is possible to think on the westward bank of the lower Kentucky River in the summer of 1998.

Over the last twenty-five or thirty years I have been making and remaking different versions of the same argument. It is not "my" argument, really, but rather one that I inherited from a long line of familial, neighborly, literary, and scientific ancestors. We could call it "the agrarian argument." This argument can be summed up in as many ways as it can be made. One way to sum it up is to say that we humans can escape neither our dependence on nature nor our responsibility to nature—and that, precisely because of this condition of dependence *and* responsibility, we are also dependent upon and responsible for human culture.

Food, as I have argued at length, is both a natural (which is to say a divine) gift and a cultural product. Because we must *use* land and water and plants and animals to produce food, we are at once dependent on and responsible to what we use. We must know both how to use and how to care for what we use. This knowledge is the basis of human culture. If we do not know how to adapt our desires, our methods, and our technology to the nature of the places in which we are working, so as to make them productive *and to keep them so*, that is a cultural failure of the grossest and most dangerous kind. Poverty and starvation also can be cultural products—if the culture is wrong.

Though this argument, in my keeping, has lengthened and acquired branches, in its main assumptions it has stayed the same. What has changed—and I say this with a good deal of wonder and with much thankfulness—is the audience. Perhaps the audience will always include people who are not listening, or people who think the agrarian argument is merely an anachronism, a form of entertainment, or a nuisance to be waved away. But increasingly the audience also includes people who take this argument seriously, because they are involved in one or more of the tasks of agrarianism. They are trying to maintain a practical foothold on the earth for themselves or their families or their communities. They are trying to preserve and develop local land-based economies. They are trying to preserve or restore the health of local communities and ecosystems and watersheds. They are opposing the attempt of the great corporations to own and control all of Creation.

In short, the agrarian argument now has a significant number of friends. As the political and ecological abuses of the so-called global economy become more noticeable and more threatening, the agrarian argument is going to have more friends than it has now. This being so, maybe the advocate's task needs to change. Maybe now, instead of merely propounding (and repeating) the agrarian argument, the advocate must also try to see that this argument does not win friends too easily. I think, myself, that this is the case. The tasks of agrarianism that we have undertaken are not going to be finished for a long time. To preserve the remnants of agrarian life, to oppose the abuses of industrial land use and finally correct them, and to develop the locally adapted economies and cultures that are necessary to our survival will require many lifetimes of dedicated work. This work does not need friends with illusions. And so I would like to speak—in a friendly way, of course—out of my distrust of "movements."

I have had with my friend Wes Jackson a number of useful conversations about the necessity of getting out of movements—even movements that have seemed necessary and dear to us—when they have lapsed into self-righteousness and self-betrayal, as movements seem almost invariably to do. People in movements too readily learn to deny to others the rights and privileges they demand for themselves. They too easily become unable to mean their own language, as when a "peace movement" becomes violent.

They often become too specialized, as if they cannot help taking refuge in the pinhole vision of the industrial intellectuals. They almost always fail to be radical enough, dealing finally in effects rather than causes. Or they deal with single issues or single solutions, as if to assure themselves that they will not be radical enough.

And so I must declare my dissatisfaction with movements to promote soil conservation or clean water or clean air or wilderness preservation or sustainable agriculture or community health or the welfare of children. Worthy as these and other goals may be, they cannot be achieved alone. They cannot be responsibly advocated alone. I am dissatisfied with such efforts because they are too specialized, they are not comprehensive enough, they are not radical enough, they virtually predict their own failure by implying that we can remedy or control effects while leaving the causes in place. Ultimately, I think, they are insincere; they propose that the trouble is caused by *other* people; they would like to change policy but not behavior.

The worst danger may be that a movement will lose its language either to its own confusion about meaning and practice, or to preemption by its enemies. I remember, for example, my naïve confusion at learning that it was possible for advocates of organic agriculture to look upon the "organic method" as an end in itself. To me, organic farming was attractive both as a way of conserving nature and as a strategy of survival for small farmers. Imagine my surprise in discovering that there could be huge "organic" monocultures. And so I was somewhat prepared for the recent attempt of the United States Department of Agriculture to appropriate the "organic" label for food irradiation, genetic engineering, and other desecrations by the corporate food economy. Once we allow our language to mean anything that anybody wants it to mean, it becomes impossible to mean what we say. When "homemade" ceases to mean neither more nor less than "made at home," then it means anything, which is to say that it means nothing. The same decay is at work on words such as "conservation," "sustainable," "safe," "natural," "healthful," "sanitary," and "organic." The use of such words now requires the most exacting control of context and the use immediately of illustrative examples.

Real organic gardeners and farmers who market their produce locally are finding that, to a lot of people, "organic" means something like "trustworthy." And so, for a while, it will be useful for us to talk about the meaning and the economic usefulness of trust and trustworthiness. But we must be careful. Sooner or later, Trust Us Global Foods, Inc., will be upon us, advertising safe, sanitary, natural food irradiation. And then we must be prepared to raise another standard and move on.

As you see, I have good reasons for declining to name the movement I think I am a part of. I call it The Nameless Movement for Better Ways of Doing—which I hope is too long and uncute to be used as a bumper sticker. I know that movements tend to die with their names and slogans, and I believe that this Nameless Movement needs to live on and on. I am reconciled to the likelihood that from time to time it will name itself and have slogans, but I am not going to use its slogans or call it by any of its names. After this, I intend to stop calling it The Nameless Movement for Better Ways of Doing, for fear it will become the NMBWD and acquire a headquarters and a budget and an inventory of T-shirts covered with language that in a few years will be mere spelling.

Let us suppose, then, that we have a Nameless Movement for Better Land Use and that we know we must try to keep it active, responsive, and intelligent for a long time. What must we do?

What we must do above all, I think, is try to see the problem in its full size and difficulty. If we are concerned about land abuse, then we must see that this is an economic problem. Every economy is, by definition, a land-using economy. If we are using our land wrong, then something is wrong with our economy. This is difficult. It becomes more difficult when we recognize that, in modern times, every one of us is a member of the economy of everybody else. Every one of us has given many proxies to the economy to use the land (and the air, the water, and other natural gifts) on our behalf. Adequately supervising those proxies is at present impossible; withdrawing them is for virtually all of us, as things now stand, unthinkable.

But if we are concerned about land abuse, we have begun an extensive work of economic criticism. Study of the history of land use (and any local history will do) informs us that we have had for a long time an economy that thrives by undermining its own foundations. Industrialism, which is the name of our economy, and which is now virtually the only economy of the world, has been from its beginnings in a state of riot. It is based squarely upon the principle of violence toward everything on which it depends, and it has not mattered whether the form of industrialism was communist or capitalist; the violence toward nature, human communities, traditional agricultures, and local economies has been constant. The bad news is coming in from all over the world. Can such an economy somehow be fixed without being radically changed? I don't think it can.

The Captains of Industry have always counseled the rest of us to "be realistic." Let us, therefore, be realistic. Is it realistic to assume that the present economy would be just fine if only it would stop poisoning the earth, air, and water, or if only it would stop soil erosion, or if only it would stop degrading watersheds and forest ecosystems, or if only it would stop seducing children, or if only it would quit buying politicians, or if only it would give women and favored minorities an equitable share of the loot? Realism, I think, is a very limited program, but it informs us at least that we should not look for bird eggs in a cuckoo clock.

Or we can show the hopelessness of single-issue causes and single-issue movements by following a line of thought such as this: We need a continuous supply of uncontaminated water. Therefore, we need (among other things) soil-and-water-conserving ways of agriculture and forestry that are not dependent on monoculture, toxic chemicals, or the indifference and violence that always accompany big-scale industrial enterprises on the land. Therefore, we need diversified, small-scale land economies that are dependent on people. Therefore, we need people with the knowledge, skills, motives, and attitudes required by diversified, small-scale land economies. And all this is clear and comfortable enough, until we recognize the question we have come to: *Where are the people?*

Well, all of us who live in the suffering rural landscapes of the United States know that most people are available to those landscapes only recreationally. We see them bicycling or boating or hiking or camping or hunting or fishing or driving along and looking around. They do not, in Mary Austin's phrase, "summer and winter with the land." They are unacquainted with the land's human and natural economies. Though people have not progressed beyond the need to eat food and drink water and wear clothes and live in houses, most people have progressed beyond the domestic arts—the husbandry and wifery of the world—by which those needful things are produced and conserved. In fact, the comparative few who still practice that necessary husbandry and wifery often are inclined to apologize for doing so, having been carefully taught in our education system that those arts are degrading and unworthy of people's talents. Educated minds, in the modern era, are unlikely to know anything about food and drink or clothing and shelter. In merely taking these things for granted, the modern educated mind reveals itself also to be as superstitious a mind as ever has existed in the world. What could be more superstitious than the idea that money brings forth food?

I am not suggesting, of course, that everybody ought to be a farmer or a forester. Heaven forbid! I *am* suggesting that most people now are living on the far side of a broken connection, and that this is potentially catastrophic. Most people are now fed, clothed, and sheltered from sources, in nature and in the work of other people, toward which they feel no gratitude and exercise no responsibility.

We are involved now in a profound failure of imagination. Most of us cannot imagine the wheat beyond the bread, or the farmer beyond the wheat, or the farm beyond the farmer, or the history (human or natural) beyond the farm. Most people cannot imagine the forest and the forest economy that produced their houses and furniture and paper; or the landscapes, the streams, and the weather that fill their pitchers and bathtubs and swimming pools with water. Most people appear to assume that when they have paid their money for these things they have entirely met their obligations. And that is, in fact, the conventional economic assumption. The problem is that it is possible to starve under the rule of the conventional economic assumption; some people are starving now under the rule of that assumption.

Money does not bring forth food. Neither does the technology of the food system. Food comes from nature and from the work of people. If the supply of food is to be continuous for a long time, then people must work in harmony with nature. That means that people must find the right answers to a lot of questions. The same rules apply to forestry and the possibility of a continuous supply of forest products.

People grow the food that people eat. People produce the lumber that people use. People care properly or improperly for the forests and the farms that are the sources of those goods. People are necessarily at both ends of the process. The economy, always obsessed with its need to sell products, thinks obsessively and exclusively of the consumer. It mostly takes for granted or ignores those who do the damaging or the restorative and preserving work of agriculture and forestry. The economy pays poorly for this work, with the unsurprising result that the work is mostly done poorly. But here we must ask a very realistic economic question: Can we afford to have this work done poorly? Those of us who know something about land stewardship know that we cannot afford to pay poorly for it, because that means simply that we will not get it. And we know that we cannot afford land use without land stewardship.

One way we could describe the task ahead of us is by saying that we need to enlarge the consciousness and the conscience of the economy. Our economy needs to know—and care—what it is doing. This is revolutionary, of course, if you have a taste for revolution, but it is also merely a matter of common sense. How could anybody seriously object to the possibility that the economy might eventually come to know what it is doing?

Undoubtedly some people will want to start a movement to bring this about. They probably will call it the Movement to Teach the Economy What It Is Doing—the MTEWIID. Despite my very considerable uneasiness, I will agree to participate, but on three conditions.

My first condition is that this movement should begin by giving up all hope and belief in piecemeal, one-shot solutions. The present scientific quest for odorless hog manure should give us sufficient proof that the specialist is no longer with us. Even now, after centuries of reductionist propaganda, the world is still intricate and vast, as dark as it is light, a place of mystery, where we cannot do one thing without doing many things, or put two things together without putting many things together. Water quality, for example, cannot be improved without improving farming and forestry, but farming and forestry cannot be improved without improving the education of consumers—and so on.

The proper business of a human economy is to make one whole thing of ourselves and this world. To make ourselves into a practical wholeness with the land under our feet is maybe not altogether possible—how would *we* know?—but, as a goal, it at least carries us beyond *hubris*, beyond the utterly groundless assumption that we can subdivide our present great failure into a thousand separate problems that can be fixed by a thousand task forces of academic and bureaucratic specialists. That program has been given more than a fair chance to prove itself, and we ought to know by now that it won't work.

My second condition is that the people in this movement (the MTE-WIID) should take full responsibility for themselves as members of the economy. If we are going to teach the economy what it is doing, then we need to learn what *we* are doing. This is going to have to be a private movement as well as a public one. If it is unrealistic to expect wasteful industries to be conservers, then obviously we must lead in part the public life of complainers, petitioners, protesters, advocates and supporters of stricter regulations and saner policies. But that is not enough. If it is unrealistic to expect a bad economy to try to become a good one, then *we* must go to work to build a good economy. It is appropriate that this duty should fall to us, for good economic behavior is more possible for us than it is for the great corporations with their miseducated managers and their greedy and oblivious stockholders. Because it is possible for us, we must try in every way we can to make good economic sense in our own lives, in our households, and in our communities. We must do more for ourselves and our neighbors. We must learn to spend our money with our friends and not with our enemies. But to do this, it is necessary to renew local economies, and revive the domestic arts. In seeking to change our economic use of the world, we are seeking inescapably to change our lives. The outward harmony that we desire between our economy and the world depends finally upon an inward harmony between our own hearts and the creative spirit that is the life of all creatures, a spirit as near us as our flesh and yet forever beyond the measures of this obsessively measuring age. We can grow good wheat and make good bread only if we understand that we do not live by bread alone.

My third condition is that this movement should content itself to be poor. We need to find cheap solutions, solutions within the reach of everybody, and the availability of a lot of money prevents the discovery of cheap solutions. The solutions of modern medicine and modern agriculture are all staggeringly expensive, and this is caused in part, and maybe altogether, by the availability of huge sums of money for medical and agricultural research.

Too much money, moreover, attracts administrators and experts as sugar attracts ants—look at what is happening in our universities. We should not envy rich movements that are organized and led by an alternative bureaucracy living on the problems it is supposed to solve. We want a movement that is a movement because it is advanced by all its members in their daily lives.

Now, having completed this very formidable list of the problems and difficulties, fears and fearful hopes that lie ahead of us, I am relieved to see that I have been preparing myself all along to end by saying something cheerful. What I have been talking about is the possibility of renewing human respect for this earth and all the good, useful, and beautiful things that come from it. I have made it clear, I hope, that I don't think this respect can be adequately enacted or conveyed by tipping our hats to nature or by representing natural loveliness in art or by prayers of thanksgiving or by preserving tracts of wilderness—though I recommend all those things. The respect I mean can be given only by using well the world's goods that are given to us. This good use, which renews respect—which is the only currency, so to speak, of respect—also renews our pleasure. The callings and disciplines that I have spoken of as the domestic arts are stationed all along the way from the farm to the prepared dinner, from the forest to the dinner table, from stewardship of the land to hospitality to friends and strangers. These arts are as demanding and gratifying, as instructive and as pleasing as the so-called fine arts. To learn them, to practice them, to honor and reward them is, I believe, our profoundest calling. Our reward is that they will enrich our lives and make us glad.

(1998)

Twelve Paragraphs
on Biotechnology

I.

I understand, from my scientific mentors and my reading, that there are two areas in which the relationship of causes and effects is highly complex: that which is internal to organisms, and that of the larger natural and human contexts—ultimately the world. In biotechnology, as in *any* technology affecting living systems, there is nothing perfectly predictable. What we do within living bodies and in the living world is never a simple mechanical procedure such as threading a needle or winding a watch. Mystery exists; unforeseen and unforeseeable consequences are common.

II.

As applied in the living world, biotechnology, like *any* technology, will be used with specific and necessarily limited intentions for specific and limited purposes. Like any technology so applied, it risks unpredicted effects; and it will have, even less predictably, what we might properly call *influences*, not only on the biological and ecological systems in which it is applied, but also on human economies, communities, and cultures.

III.

It is therefore not surprising that the criticism of the work so far of the biotechnologists has begun with the accusation that in their publicity and advertising their science has been seriously oversimplified, and thus made available for the same sort of aggressive mass marketing that sells breakfast cereal.

IV.

Biotechnology, as practiced so far, is bad science—a science willingly disdainful or ignorant of the ecological and human costs of previous scientific-technological revolutions (such as the introduction of chemistry into agriculture), and disdainful of criticism within the scientific disciplines. It is, moreover, a science involved directly with product-development, marketing, and political lobbying on behalf of the products—and, therefore, is directly corruptible by personal self-interest and greed. For such a science to present itself in the guise of objectivity or philanthropy is, at best, hypocritical.

V.

Further problems arise when we consider biotechnology as an "agribusiness." As such, its effect will be to complete the long-established program of industry in agriculture, which has been to eliminate the ecological and cultural "givens": natural fertility, solar energy, local genetics, agronomic weed and pest control, animal husbandry—and now the entire genetic commonwealth. The aim, in short, is to require *every* farmer to come to a corporate supplier for *every* need.

VI.

As a science specifically agricultural, biotechnology would enlarge, and worsen, another problem related to the industrialization of farming: that is, the failure to adapt the farming to the land. In agricultural biotechnology, as in industrial agriculture generally, the inevitable emphasis is upon uniformity—in crop varieties, livestock breeds, methodologies, animal carcasses, and so on.

VII.

But as local adaptation is the inescapable requirement for the survival of species, so is it the indispensable criterion for an enduring agriculture. Ultimately, the problems of agriculture—as such, not as an industry—will be solved on farms, farm by farm, not in laboratories or factories. And so we must regard every proposed industrial solution to an agricultural problem—including biotechnology—as potentially a distraction from the real problem and an obstacle to the real solution.

VIII.

Finally, to do full justice to this issue, we must consider the likelihood that genetic engineering is not just a science, a technology, and a business but is also an intellectual fad and to some extent an economic bubble. It is being sold, and therefore oversold, as the latest answer-to-everything: It will solve the problem of hunger; it will cure every disease; it will "engineer our emotions, to make us happy and content all the time" (even, presumably, when we are broke, friendless, and have been hit by a car); it will permit everybody's genome to be "read" in a sort of new-age palmistry. It is swarmed about by speculators and by what Sharon Kardia of the University of Michigan calls "snake oil salesmen."

IX.

Biotechnology also is extremely expensive in comparison to conventional plant breeding and is costly to farmers. Some biotechnology companies are begging for money, while others are *giving* huge grants to university microbiology departments. The industry's attitude toward farmers is hostile, as demonstrated by its lawsuits against them and its pursuit of the "terminator gene." Its attitude toward consumers is aggressive and contemptuous, as demonstrated by its campaign against labeling.

X.

The biotechnology industry is thus founded on questionable science, is ethically obscure, is economically uncertain; it involves unconfronted dangers to the natural world and human health, and its economic benefit to farmers or to food production has not been demonstrated. It is the sort of gamble typically attractive to corporate investors and venture capitalists, who in fact have supported it lavishly. Any biotechnology enterprise that fails to attract sufficient funds from those sources should be considered to have failed a critical test. Such an enterprise cannot responsibly be bailed out with public funds or with funds dedicated to the relief of distressed farm-ers. To do so would be, in effect, to levy a tax for the support of a private business. It would be a breach of trust.

XI.

Richard Strohman, of the University of California–Berkeley, has proposed that the problems of biotechnology arise, not because the science is new, but because it is old. He sees it as a development of a now outdated paradigm according to which scientists have undertaken to supply simple solutions to complex problems, without due regard to the complexity of the problems. The proper scientific response to this, he says, is to enlarge the context of the work.

XII.

If biotechnology is not a sufficient, or even an adequate, answer to agricul-tural problems, then what do we need? My own answer is that we need a science of agriculture that is authentically new—a science that freely and generously accepts the farm, the local ecosystem, and the local community as contexts, and then devotes itself to the relationship between farming and its ecological and cultural supports.

(2002)

Let the Farm Judge

To me, one of the most informative books on agriculture is *British Sheep,* published by the National Sheep Association of Britain. This book contains photographs and descriptions of sixty-five British sheep breeds and "recognized half-breds." I have spent a good deal of time looking at the pictures in this book and reading its breed descriptions, for I think that it represents one of the great accomplishments of agriculture. It makes a most impressive case for the intelligence and the judgment of British farmers over many centuries.

What does it mean that an island not much bigger than Kansas or not much more than twice the size of Kentucky should have developed sixty or so breeds of sheep? It means that many thousands of farmers were paying the most discriminating attention, not only to their sheep, but also to the nature of their local landscapes and economies, for a long time. They were responding intelligently to the requirement of local adaptation. The result, when such an effort is carried on by enough intelligent farmers in the same region for a long time, is the development of a distinct breed that fits regional needs. Such local adaptation is the most important requirement for agriculture, wherever it occurs. If you are going to adapt your farming to a variety of landscapes, you are going to need a variety of livestock breeds, and a variety of types within breeds.

The great diversity of livestock breeds, along with the great diversity of domestic plant varieties, can be thought of as a sort of vocabulary with which we may make appropriate responses to the demands of a great diversity of localities. The goal of intelligent farmers, who desire the long-term success of farming, is to adapt their work to their places. Local adaptation always requires reasonably correct answers to *two* questions: What is the nature— the need and the opportunity—of the local economy? and, What is the nature of the place? For example, it is a mistake to answer the economic question by plowing too steep a hillside, just as it is a mistake to answer the geographic or ecological question in a way that denies the farmer a living.

Intelligent livestock breeders may find that, in practice, the two questions become one: How can I produce the best meat at the lowest economic and ecological cost? This question cannot be satisfactorily answered by the market, by the meatpacking industry, by breed societies, or by show ring judges. It cannot be answered satisfactorily by "animal science" experts, or by genetic engineers. It can only be answered satisfactorily by the farmer, and only if the farm, the place itself, is allowed to play a part in the process of selection.

It goes without saying that the animal finally produced by any farm will be a product to some extent of the judgment of the farmer, the meatpacker, the breed society, and the show ring judge. But the farm too must be permitted to make and enforce its judgment. If it is not permitted to do so, then there can be no local adaptation. And where there is no local adaptation, the farmer and the farm must pay significant penalties.

In our era, because of commercial demand and the allure of the show ring, livestock breeding has tended to concentrate on the production of outstanding individual animals as determined by the ideal breed characteristics or the ideal carcass. In other words, a good brood cow or ewe is one that produces offspring that fit the prevailing show or commercial standards. We don't worry enough about the *cost* of production, which would lead us directly to the issue of local adaptation. This sort of negligence, I think, could have been possible only in our time, when "cheap" fossil fuel has set the pattern in agriculture. Suffice it to say that much thoughtlessness in livestock breeding has been subsidized by large checks paid to veterinarians and drug companies, and covered over by fat made of allegedly cheap corn.

Allegedly cheap fossil fuel, allegedly cheap transportation, and allegedly cheap corn and other feed grains have pushed agriculture toward uniformity, obscuring regional differences and, with them, the usefulness of locally adapted breeds, especially those that do well on forages. This is why there are now only a few dominant breeds, and why those breeds are large and grain-dependent. Now, for example, nearly all dairy cows are Holsteins, and the modern sheep is more than likely to have a black face and to be "big and tall."

My friend Maury Telleen has pointed out to me that fifty years ago the Ayrshire was a popular dairy cow in New England and Kansas. The reason was her ability to make milk on the feed that was locally available; she did not require the optimal conditions and feedstuffs of Iowa or Illinois. She was, Maury says, "a cow that could 'get along.'" It is dangerous to assume that we have got beyond the need for farm animals that can "get along."

If we assume that the inescapable goal of the farmer, especially in the present economy, must be to reduce costs, and, further, that costs are reduced by local adaptation, then we can begin to think about the problems of livestock breeding by noting that corn, whatever its market price, is not cheap. What is cheap is grass—*grazed* grass—and where the grass grows determines the kind of animal needed to graze it.

Our farm, in the lower Kentucky River valley, is mostly on hillsides. Heavy animals tend to damage hillsides, especially in winter. Our experience with brood cows showed us that our farm needs sheep. It needs, in addition, sheep that can make their living by grazing coarse pasture on hillsides. And so in the fall of 1978 we bought six Border Cheviot ewes and a buck. At present we have about thirty ewes, and eventually we will have more.

Our choice of breed was a good one. The Border Cheviot is a hill sheep, developed to make good use of such rough pasture as we have. Moreover, it can make good use of a little corn, and our farm is capable of producing a little corn. There have been problems, of course. Some of them have had to do with adapting ourselves to our breed. These have been important, but just as important have been the problems of adapting our flock to our farm. And those are the problems I want to discuss.

There are now probably more Cheviots in the Midwest than elsewhere in the United States. For us, at any rate, the inevitable source of breeding stock has been the Midwest, and many of our problems have been traceable to that fact. What I am going to say implies no fault in the Midwestern breeders, to whom we and our breed have an enormous debt. It is nevertheless true that, for a flock of sheep, living is easier in the prairie lands than on a Kentucky hillside. Just walking around on a hillside farm involves more strain and requires more energy, and the less fertile the land the farther a ewe will have to walk to fill her belly. Knees that might have remained sound on the gentle topography of Ohio or Iowa may become arthritic at our place. Also a ewe that would have twin lambs on a prairie farm may have only one on a hill farm. Similarly, a lamb will grow to slaughter weight more slowly where he has to allocate more energy to getting around. We once sold five yearling ewes to our friend Bob Willerton in Danvers, Illinois, where on their first lambing they produced eleven lambs. On our farm, they *might* have produced seven or eight. We have noticed the same difference with cull ewes that we have sent to our son's farm, which is less steep and more fertile than ours.

Our farm, then, is asking for a ewe that can stay healthy, live long, breed successfully, have two lambs without assistance, and feed them well, in comparatively demanding circumstances. Experience has shown us that the Border Cheviot breed is capable of producing a ewe of this kind, but that it does not do so inevitably. In eighteen years, and out of a good many ewes bought or raised, we have identified so far only two ewe families (the female descendents of two ewes) that fairly dependably perform as we and our place require.

The results of identifying and keeping the daughters of these ewe families have been very satisfactory. This year they made up more than half of our bred ewes. Presumably because of that, our lambing percentage, which previously hovered around 150 percent, increased to 172 percent. This year also we reduced our winter hay-feeding by one month, not beginning until the first of February. Next year, we hope to feed no hay until we bring the ewes to the barn for lambing, which will be about the first of March.[1] In livestock breeding it is always too early to brag, but of course we are encouraged.

In the language of Phillip Sponenberg and Carolyn Christman's excellent *Conservation Breeding Handbook,* we have employed "extensive" or "landrace" husbandry in managing a standardized breed. From the first, our flock has been "challenged by the environment"—required to live on what the place can most cheaply and sustainably provide, mainly pasture, with a minimum of attention and virtually no professional veterinary care. We give selenium injections to ewes and lambs and use a prudent amount of medication for parasites. We give no inoculations except for tetanus to the newborn lambs, and we have never trimmed a hoof.

Until recently, and even now with ewes, our practice has been to buy bargains, animals that for one reason or another fell below the standards of the show ring. But I don't believe that our flock would have developed to our standards and requirements any faster if we had bought the champions out of the best shows every year. Some of the qualities we were after simply are not visible to show ring judges.

I am not trying to argue that there is no good in livestock shows. The

---

1. We did so the next year, and have continued to do so, except in times of deep or crusted snow. We winter our ewes on a hillside that is ungrazed from early August until about Christmas.

show ring is a useful tool; it is obviously instructive when good breeders bring good animals together for comparison. I am saying only that the show ring alone cannot establish and maintain adequate standards for livestock breeders. You could not develop locally adapted strains if your only standards came from the show ring or from breed societies.

The point is that, especially now when grain-feeding and confinement-feeding are so common, no American breeder should expect any *breed* to be locally adapted. Breeders should recognize that from the standpoint of local adaptation and cheap production, every purchase of a breeding animal is a gamble. A newly purchased ewe or buck may improve the performance of your flock on your farm or it may not. Good breeders will know, or they will soon find out, that theirs is not the only judgment that is involved. While the breeder is judging, the breeder's farm also is judging, enforcing its demands, and making selections. And this is as it should be. The judgment of the farm serves the breed, helping to preserve its genetic diversity.

Because of the necessity of purchasing sires from time to time, the continuity of the locally adapted flock must reside in the female lineages. Studying and preserving the most long-lived, thrifty, and productive ewe families is paramount. But this need not be laborious, for your farm will be selecting along with you. You pick the individuals that look good. This always implies that they have done well; and sooner or later you will know the look of "your kind," the kind that is apt to do well on your place. Your farm, however, will pick the ones that last. Even if you do not select at all, or if you select wrongly, a ewe that is not fitted to your farm will not contribute as many breeding animals to your flock as will a ewe that *is* fitted to your farm.

It is generally acknowledged that a shepherd should know what he or she is doing. It is not so generally understood that the flock should know what *it* is doing—that is, how to live, thrive, and reproduce successfully on its home farm. But this knowledge, bred into the flock, is critical; it means meat from grass, at the lowest cost.

(1997)

The Total Economy

———————— ❧ ————————

L ET US BEGIN by assuming what appears to be true: that the so-called environmental crisis is now pretty well established as a fact of our age. The problems of pollution, species extinction, loss of wilderness, loss of farmland, and loss of topsoil may still be ignored or scoffed at, but they are not denied. Concern for these problems has acquired a certain standing, a measure of discussability, in the media and in some scientific, academic, and religious institutions.

This is good, of course; obviously, we can't hope to solve these problems without an increase of public awareness and concern. But in an age burdened with "publicity," we have to be aware also that as issues rise into popularity they rise also into the danger of oversimplification. To speak of this danger is especially necessary in confronting the destructiveness of our relationship to nature, which is the result, in the first place, of gross oversimplification.

The "environmental crisis" has happened because the human household or economy is in conflict at almost every point with the household of nature. We have built our household on the assumption that the natural household is simple and can be simply used. We have assumed increasingly over the last five hundred years that nature is merely a supply of "raw materials," and that we may safely possess those materials merely by taking them. This taking, as our technical means have increased, has involved always less reverence or respect, less gratitude, less local knowledge, and less skill. Our methodologies of land use have strayed from our old sympathetic attempts to imitate natural processes, and have come more and more to resemble the methodology of mining, even as mining itself has become more powerful technologically and more brutal.

And so we will be wrong if we attempt to correct what we perceive as "environmental" problems without correcting the economic oversimplification that caused them. This oversimplification is now either a matter of corporate behavior or of behavior under the influence of corporate behavior. This is sufficiently clear to many of us. What is not sufficiently clear, perhaps to any of us, is the extent of our complicity, as individuals and especially as individual consumers, in the behavior of the corporations.

What has happened is that most people in our country, and apparently most people in the "developed" world, have given proxies to the corporations to produce and provide *all* of their food, clothing, and shelter. Moreover, they are rapidly increasing their proxies to corporations or governments to provide entertainment, education, child care, care of the sick and the elderly, and many other kinds of "service" that once were carried on informally and inexpensively by individuals or households or communities. Our major economic practice, in short, is to delegate the practice to others.

The danger now is that those who are concerned will believe that the solution to the "environmental crisis" can be merely political—that the problems, being large, can be solved by large solutions generated by a few people to whom we will give our proxies to police the economic proxies that we have already given. The danger, in other words, is that people will think they have made a sufficient change if they have altered their "values," or had a "change of heart," or experienced a "spiritual awakening," and that such a change in passive consumers will necessarily cause appropriate changes in the public experts, politicians, and corporate executives to whom they have granted their political and economic proxies.

The trouble with this is that a proper concern for nature and our use of nature must be practiced, not by our proxy-holders, but by ourselves. A change of heart or of values without a practice is only another pointless luxury of a passively consumptive way of life. The "environmental crisis," in fact, can be solved only if people, individually and in their communities, recover responsibility for their thoughtlessly given proxies. If people begin the effort to take back into their own power a significant portion of their economic responsibility, then their inevitable first discovery is that the "environmental crisis" is no such thing; it is not a crisis of our environs or surroundings; it is a crisis of our lives as individuals, as family members, as community members, and as citizens. We have an "environmental crisis" because *we* have consented to an economy in which by eating, drinking, working, resting, traveling, and enjoying ourselves we are destroying the natural, the God-given, world.

We live, as we must sooner or later recognize, in an era of sentimental economics and, consequently, of sentimental politics. Sentimental communism holds in effect that everybody and everything should suffer for the good of "the many" who, though miserable in the present, will be happy in the future for exactly the same reasons that they are miserable in the present.

Sentimental capitalism is not so different from sentimental communism as the corporate and political powers claim to suppose. Sentimental capitalism holds in effect that everything small, local, private, personal, natural, good, and beautiful must be sacrificed in the interest of the "free market" and the great corporations, which will bring unprecedented security and happiness to "the many"—in, of course, the future.

These forms of political economy may be described as sentimental because they depend absolutely upon a political faith for which there is no justification. They seek to preserve the gullibility of the people by issuing a cold check on a fund of political virtue that does not exist. Communism and "free-market" capitalism both are modern versions of oligarchy. In their propaganda, both justify violent means by good ends, which always are put beyond reach by the violence of the means. The trick is to define the end vaguely—"the greatest good of the greatest number" or "the benefit of the many"—and keep it at a distance. For example, the United States government's agricultural policy, or non-policy, since 1952 has merely consented to the farmers' predicament of high costs and low prices; it has never envisioned or advocated in particular the prosperity of farmers or of farmland, but has only promised "cheap food" to consumers and "survival" to the "larger and more efficient" farmers who supposedly could adapt to and endure the attrition of high costs and low prices. And after each inevitable wave of farm failures and the inevitable enlargement of the destitution and degradation of the countryside, there have been the inevitable reassurances from government propagandists and university experts that American agriculture was now more efficient and that everybody would be better off in the future.

The fraudulence of these oligarchic forms of economy is in their principle of displacing whatever good they recognize (as well as their debts) from the present to the future. Their success depends upon persuading people, first, that whatever they have now is no good, and, second, that the promised good is certain to be achieved in the future. This obviously contradicts the principle—common, I believe, to all the religious traditions—that if ever we are going to do good to one another, then the time to do it is now; we are to receive no reward for promising to do it in the future. And both communism and capitalism have found such principles to be a great embarrassment. If you are presently occupied in destroying every good thing in sight in order to do good in the future, it is inconvenient to have people saying things like "Love thy neighbor as thyself" or "Sentient beings are numberless, I vow to save them." Communists and capitalists alike, "liberal" capitalists and "conservative" capitalists alike, have needed to replace religion with some form of determinism, so that they can say to their victims, "I'm doing this because I can't do otherwise. It is not my fault. It is inevitable." This is a lie, obviously, and religious organizations have too often consented to it.

The idea of an economy based upon several kinds of ruin may seem a contradiction in terms, but in fact such an economy is possible, as we see. It is possible, however, on one implacable condition: The only future good that it assuredly leads to is that it will destroy itself. And how does it disguise this outcome from its subjects, its short-term beneficiaries, and its victims? It does so by false accounting. It substitutes for the real economy, by which we build and maintain (or do not maintain) our household, a symbolic economy of money, which in the long run, because of the self-interested manipulations of the "controlling interests," cannot symbolize or account for anything but itself. And so we have before us the spectacle of unprecedented "prosperity" and "economic growth" in a land of degraded farms, forests, ecosystems, and watersheds, polluted air, failing families, and perishing communities.

This moral and economic absurdity exists for the sake of the allegedly "free" market, the single principle of which is this: Commodities will be produced wherever they can be produced at the lowest cost and consumed wherever they will bring the highest price. To make too cheap and sell too high has always been the program of industrial capitalism. The global "free market" is merely capitalism's so far successful attempt to enlarge the geographic scope of its greed, and moreover to give to its greed the status of a "right" within its presumptive territory. The global "free market" is free to the corporations precisely because it dissolves the boundaries of the old national colonialisms, and replaces them with a new colonialism without restraints or boundaries. It is pretty much as if all the rabbits have now been forbidden to have holes, thereby "freeing" the hounds.

The "right" of a corporation to exercise its economic power without restraint is construed, by the partisans of the "free market," as a form of freedom, a political liberty implied presumably by the right of individual citizens to own and use property.

But the "free market" idea introduces into government a sanction of an inequality that is not implicit in any idea of democratic liberty: namely that the "free market" is freest to those who have the most money, and is not free at all to those with little or no money. Wal-Mart, for example, as a large corporation "freely" competing against local, privately owned businesses, has virtually all the freedom, and its small competitors virtually none.

To make too cheap and sell too high, there are two requirements. One is that you must have a lot of consumers with surplus money and unlimited wants. For the time being, there are plenty of these consumers in the "developed" countries. The problem, for the time being easily solved, is simply to keep them relatively affluent and dependent on purchased supplies.

The other requirement is that the market for labor and raw materials should remain depressed relative to the market for retail commodities. This means that the supply of workers should exceed demand, and that the land-using economies should be allowed or encouraged to overproduce.

To keep the cost of labor low, it is necessary first to entice or force country people everywhere in the world to move into the cities—in the manner prescribed by the Committee for Economic Development after World War II—and, second, to continue to introduce labor-replacing technology. In this way it is possible to maintain a "pool" of people who are in the threatful position of being mere consumers, landless and poor, and who therefore are eager to go to work for low wages—precisely the condition of migrant farm workers in the United States.

To cause the land-using economies to overproduce is even simpler. The farmers and other workers in the world's land-using economies, by and large, are not organized. They are therefore unable to control production in order to secure just prices. Individual producers must go individually to the market and take for their produce simply whatever they are paid. They have no power to bargain or to make demands. Increasingly, they must sell, not to neighbors or to neighboring towns and cities, but to large and remote corporations. There is no competition among the buyers (supposing there is more than one), who *are* organized and are "free" to exploit the advantage of low prices. Low prices encourage overproduction, as producers attempt to make up their losses "on volume," and overproduction inevitably makes for low prices. The land-using economies thus spiral downward as the money economy of the exploiters spirals upward. If economic attrition in the land-using population becomes so severe as to threaten production, then governments can subsidize production without production controls, which necessarily will encourage overproduction, which will lower prices—and so the subsidy to rural producers becomes, in effect, a subsidy to the purchasing corporations. In the land-using economies, production is further cheapened by destroying, with low prices and low standards of quality, the cultural imperatives for good work and land stewardship.

This sort of exploitation, long familiar in the foreign and domestic colonialism of modern nations, has now become "the global economy," which is the property of a few supranational corporations. The economic theory used to justify the global economy in its "free market" version is, again, perfectly groundless and sentimental. The idea is that what is good for the corporations will sooner or later—though not of course immediately—be good for everybody.

That sentimentality is based, in turn, upon a fantasy: the proposition that the great corporations, in "freely" competing with one another for raw materials, labor, and market share, will drive each other indefinitely, not only toward greater "efficiencies" of manufacture, but also toward higher bids for raw materials and labor and lower prices to consumers. As a result, all the world's people will be economically secure—in the future. It would be hard to object to such a proposition if only it were true.

But one knows, in the first place, that "efficiency" in manufacture always means reducing labor costs by replacing workers with cheaper workers or with machines.

In the second place, the "law of competition" does *not* imply that many competitors will compete indefinitely. The law of competition is a simple paradox: Competition destroys competition. The law of competition implies that many competitors, competing on the "free market" without restraint, will ultimately and inevitably reduce the number of competitors to one. The law of competition, in short, is the law of war.

In the third place, the global economy is based upon cheap long-distance transportation, without which it is not possible to move goods from the point of cheapest origin to the point of highest sale. And cheap long-distance transportation is the basis of the idea that regions and nations should abandon any measure of economic self-sufficiency in order to specialize in production for export of the few commodities, or the single commodity, that can be most cheaply produced. Whatever may be said for the "efficiency" of such a system, its result (and, I assume, its purpose) is to destroy local production capacities, local diversity, and local economic independence. It destroys the economic security that it promises to make.

This idea of a global "free market" economy, despite its obvious moral flaws and its dangerous practical weaknesses, is now the ruling orthodoxy of the age. Its propaganda is subscribed to and distributed by most political leaders, editorial writers, and other "opinion makers." The powers that be, while continuing to budget huge sums for "national defense," have apparently abandoned any idea of national or local self-sufficiency, even in food. They also have given up the idea that a national or local government might justly place restraints upon economic activity in order to protect its land and its people.

The global economy is now institutionalized in the World Trade Organization, which was set up, without election anywhere, to rule international trade on behalf of the "free market"—which is to say on behalf of the supranational corporations—and to *overrule*, in secret sessions, any national or regional law that conflicts with the "free market." The corporate program of global "free trade" and the presence of the World Trade Organization have legitimized extreme forms of expert thought. We are told confidently that if Kentucky loses its milk-producing capacity to Wisconsin (and if Wisconsin's is lost to California), that will be a "success story." Experts such as Stephen C. Blank, of the University of California, Davis, have recommended that "developed" countries, such as the United States and the United Kingdom, where food can no longer be produced cheaply enough, should give up agriculture altogether.

The folly at the root of this foolish economy began with the idea that a corporation should be regarded, legally, as "a person." But the limitless destructiveness of this economy comes about precisely because a corporation is *not* a person. A corporation, essentially, is a pile of money to which a number of persons have sold their moral allegiance. Unlike a person, a corporation does not age. It does not arrive, as most persons finally do, at a realization of the shortness and smallness of human lives; it does not come to see the future as the lifetime of the children and grandchildren of anybody in particular. It can experience no personal hope or remorse, no change of heart. It cannot humble itself. It goes about its business as if it were immortal, with the single purpose of becoming a bigger pile of money. The stockholders essentially are usurers, people who "let their money work for them," expecting high pay in return for causing others to work for low pay. The World Trade Organization enlarges the old idea of the corporation-as-person by giving the global corporate economy the status of a super-government with the power to overrule nations.

I don't mean to say, of course, that all corporate executives and stockholders are bad people. I am only saying that all of them are very seriously implicated in a bad economy.

Unsurprisingly, among people who wish to preserve things other than money—for instance, every region's native capacity to produce essential goods—there is a growing perception that the global "free market" economy is inherently an enemy to the natural world, to human health and freedom, to industrial workers, and to farmers and others in the land-use economies; and, furthermore, that it is inherently an enemy to good work and good economic practice.

I believe that this perception is correct and that it can be shown to be correct merely by listing the assumptions implicit in the idea that corporations should be "free" to buy low and sell high in the world at large. These assumptions, so far as I can make them out, are as follows:

1. That there is no conflict between the "free market" and political freedom, and no connection between political democracy and economic democracy.

2. That there can be no conflict between economic advantage and economic justice.

3. That there is no conflict between greed and ecological or bodily health.

4. That there is no conflict between self-interest and public service.

5. That it is all right for a nation's or a region's subsistence to be foreign-based, dependent on long-distance transport, and entirely controlled by corporations.

6. That the loss or destruction of the capacity anywhere to produce necessary goods does not matter and involves no cost.

7. That, therefore, wars over commodities—our recent Gulf War, for example—are legitimate and permanent economic functions.

8. That this sort of sanctioned violence is justified also by the predominance of centralized systems of production, supply, communications, and transportation which are extremely vulnerable not only to acts of war between nations, but also to sabotage and terrorism.

9. That it is all right for poor people in poor countries to work at poor wages to produce goods for export to affluent people in rich countries.

10. That there is no danger and no cost in the proliferation of exotic pests, vermin, weeds, and diseases that accompany international trade, and that increase with the volume of trade.

11. That an economy is a machine, of which people are merely the interchangeable parts. One has no choice but to do the work (if any) that the economy prescribes, and to accept the prescribed wage.

12. That, therefore, vocation is a dead issue. One does not do the work that one chooses to do because one is called to it by Heaven or by one's natural abilities, but does instead the work that is determined and imposed by the economy. Any work is all right as long as one gets paid for it. (This assumption explains the prevailing "liberal" and "conservative" indifference toward displaced workers, farmers, and small-business people.)

13. That stable and preserving relationships among people, places, and things do not matter and are of no worth.

14. That cultures and religions have no legitimate practical or economic concerns.

These assumptions clearly prefigure a condition of total economy. A total economy is one in which everything—"life forms," for instance, or the "right to pollute"—is "private property" and has a price and is for sale. In a total economy, significant and sometimes critical choices that once belonged to individuals or communities become the property of corporations. A total economy, operating internationally, necessarily shrinks the powers of state and national governments, not only because those governments have signed over significant powers to an international bureaucracy or because political leaders become the paid hacks of the corporations, but also because political processes—and especially democratic processes—are too slow to react to unrestrained economic and technological development on a global scale. And when state and national governments begin to act in effect as agents of the global economy, selling their people for low wages and their people's products for low prices, then the rights and liberties of citizenship must necessarily shrink. A total economy is an unrestrained taking of profits from the disintegration of nations, communities, households, landscapes, and ecosystems. It licenses symbolic or artificial wealth to "grow" by means of the destruction of the real wealth of all the world.

Among the many costs of the total economy, the loss of the principle of vocation is probably the most symptomatic and, from a cultural standpoint, the most critical. It is by the replacement of vocation with economic determinism that the exterior workings of a total economy destroy human character and culture also from the inside.

In an essay on the origin of civilization in traditional cultures, Ananda Coomaraswamy wrote that "the principle of justice is the same throughout. . . . . [It is] that each member of the community should perform the task for which he is fitted by nature. . . ." The two ideas, justice and vocation, are inseparable. That is why Coomaraswamy spoke of industrialism as "the mammon of injustice," incompatible with civilization. It is by way of the practice of vocation that sanctity and reverence enter into the human economy. It was thus possible for traditional cultures to conceive that "to work is to pray."

Aware of industrialism's potential for destruction, as well as the considerable political danger of great concentrations of wealth and power in industrial corporations, American leaders developed, and for a while used, certain means of limiting and restraining such concentrations, and of somewhat equitably distributing wealth and property. The means were: laws against trusts and monopolies, the principle of collective bargaining, the concept of 100 percent parity between the land-using and the manufacturing economies, and the progressive income tax. And to protect domestic producers and production capacities, it is possible for governments to impose tariffs on cheap imported goods. These means are justified by the government's obligation to protect the lives, livelihoods, and freedoms of its citizens. There is, then, no necessity that requires our government to sacrifice the livelihoods of our small farmers, small-business people, and workers, along with our domestic economic independence, to the global "free market." But now all of these means are either weakened or in disuse. The global economy is intended as a means of subverting them.

In default of government protections against the total economy of the supranational corporations, people are where they have been many times before: in danger of losing their economic security and their freedom, both at once. But at the same time the means of defending themselves belongs to them in the form of a venerable principle: Powers not exercised by government return to the people. If the government does not propose to protect the lives, the livelihoods, and the freedoms of its people, then the people must think about protecting themselves.

How are they to protect themselves? There seems, really, to be only one way, and that is to develop and put into practice the idea of a local economy—something that growing numbers of people are now doing. For several good reasons, they are beginning with the idea of a local food economy. People are trying to find ways to shorten the distance between producers and consumers, to make the connections between the two more direct, and to make this local economic activity a benefit to the local community. They are trying to learn to use the consumer economies of local towns and cities to preserve the livelihoods of local farm families and farm communities. They want to use the local economy to give consumers an influence over the kind and quality of their food, and to preserve and enhance the local landscapes. They want to give everybody in the local community a direct, long-term interest in the prosperity, health, and beauty of their homeland. This is the only way presently available to make the total economy less total. It was once the only way to make a national or a colonial economy less total, but now the necessity is greater.

I am assuming that there is a valid line of thought leading from the idea of the total economy to the idea of a local economy. I assume that the first thought may be a recognition of one's ignorance and vulnerability as a consumer in the total economy. As such a consumer, one does not know the history of the products one uses. Where, exactly, did they come from? Who produced them? What toxins were used in their production? What were the human and ecological costs of producing and then of disposing of them? One sees that such questions cannot be answered easily, and perhaps not at all. Though one is shopping amid an astonishing variety of products, one is denied certain significant choices. In such a state of economic ignorance it is not possible to choose products that were produced locally or with reasonable kindness toward people and toward nature. Nor is it possible for such consumers to influence production for the better. Consumers who feel a prompting toward land stewardship find that in this economy they can have no stewardly practice. To be a consumer in the total economy, one must agree to be totally ignorant, totally passive, and totally dependent on distant supplies and self-interested suppliers.

And then, perhaps, one begins to *see* from a local point of view. One begins to ask, What is here, what is in my neighborhood, what is in me, that can lead to something better? From a local point of view, one can see that a global "free market" economy is possible only if nations and localities accept or ignore the inherent weakness of a production economy based on exports and a consumer economy based on imports. An export economy is beyond local influence, and so is an import economy. And cheap long-distance transport is possible only if granted cheap fuel, international peace, control of terrorism, prevention of sabotage, and the solvency of the international economy.

Perhaps also one begins to see the difference between a small local business that must share the fate of the local community and a large absentee corporation that is set up to escape the fate of the local community by ruining the local community.

So far as I can see, the idea of a local economy rests upon only two principles: neighborhood and subsistence.

In a viable neighborhood, neighbors ask themselves what they can do or provide for one another, and they find answers that they and their place can afford. This, and nothing else, is the *practice* of neighborhood. This practice must be, in part, charitable, but it must also be economic, and the economic part must be equitable; there is a significant charity in just prices.

Of course, everything needed locally cannot be produced locally. But a viable neighborhood is a community, and a viable community is made up of neighbors who cherish and protect what they have in common. This is the principle of subsistence. A viable community, like a viable farm, protects its own production capacities. It does not import products that it can produce for itself. And it does not export local products until local needs have been met. The economic products of a viable community are understood either as belonging to the community's subsistence or as surplus, and only the surplus is considered to be marketable abroad. A community, if it is to be viable, cannot think of producing solely for export, and it cannot permit importers to use cheaper labor and goods from other places to destroy the local capacity to produce goods that are needed locally. In charity, moreover, it must refuse to import goods that are produced at the cost of human or ecological degradation elsewhere. This principle of subsistence applies not just to localities, but to regions and nations as well.

The principles of neighborhood and subsistence will be disparaged by the globalists as "protectionism"—and that is exactly what it is. It is a protectionism that is just and sound, because it protects local producers and is the best assurance of adequate supplies to local consumers. And the idea that local needs should be met first and only surpluses exported does *not* imply any prejudice against charity toward people in other places or trade with them. The principle of neighborhood at home always implies the principle of charity abroad. And the principle of subsistence is in fact the best guarantee of giveable or marketable surpluses. This kind of protection is not "isolationism."

Albert Schweitzer, who knew well the economic situation in the colonies of Africa, wrote about seventy years ago: "Whenever the timber trade is good, permanent famine reigns in the Ogowe region, because the villagers abandon their farms to fell as many trees as possible." We should notice especially that the goal of production was "as many . . . as possible." And Schweitzer made my point exactly: "These people could achieve true wealth if they could develop their agriculture and trade to meet their own needs." Instead they produced timber for export to "the world market," which made them dependent upon imported goods that they bought with money earned from their exports. They gave up their local means of subsistence, and imposed the false standard of a foreign demand ("as many trees as possible") upon their forests. They thus became helplessly dependent on an economy over which they had no control.

Such was the fate of the native people under the African colonialism of Schweitzer's time. Such is, and can only be, the fate of everybody under the global colonialism of our time. Schweitzer's description of the colonial economy of the Ogowe region is in principle not different from the rural economy in Kentucky or Iowa or Wyoming now. A total economy, for all practical purposes, is a total government. The "free trade," which from the standpoint of the corporate economy brings "unprecedented economic growth," from the standpoint of the land and its local populations, and ultimately from the standpoint of the cities, is destruction and slavery. Without prosperous local economies, the people have no power and the land no voice.

(2000)

A Long Job, Too Late to Quit

B Y NOW, it is altogether too easy to diagram the modern story of a rural
community. We know the invariable downward steps of that story:

- Loss of net income to farmers in the ever-tightening strain
  between increasing costs and decreasing prices.

- Loss of jobs as a result of the continuing industrialization of
  agriculture—which is both a cause and an effect of the loss of
  population.

- Loss of self-respect among farmers as their incomes decline, and
  as they see themselves less and less respected by the people
  whom they have provided with allegedly "cheap" food.

- Loss of farms.

- Loss of dealerships, repair shops, and stores.

- Loss of local schools, churches, and other community institutions.

- Loss of political representation.

- Loss of doctors and other professionals.

- Loss of the subsistence economies, which kept the country people going through earlier hard times.

This is the history of rural communities not just in the United States, but
all over the world, and it has been going on for half a century.

The rural people who remain in the rural communities and economies are
always traveling farther and paying more for essential goods and services.
Some of these goods and services once were provided by their own farms,

families, and communities as a matter of course and at no monetary cost.
The country communities are thus always more vulnerable to the economic
shifts and trends that are never in their control or in their favor. And those
of us who have observed closely the life of a rural community know that
there comes a point in this history of loss and decline when the community
begins to choose against its own best interest—against itself. Starting perhaps in small ways, a small purchase here and there, people begin to prefer
to do business away from home. They choose Kroger over the local grocery,
and Rite Aid over the local drugstore, and Wal-Mart over a whole set of
local shops. And in doing so they choose, ultimately, against themselves. I
remember speaking with the owner of a small independent drugstore who
told me that he had seen his customers drifting away to the chain stores, but
he said they remained *his* faithful customers when they needed medicine late
at night. That is to say that they were members of "the market economy"
when they were looking for a bargain, but they returned to membership in
the local community when they needed a neighbor—a fickleness that obviously cannot be kept up indefinitely. For farmers, likewise, the stretch is
always longer and tighter between the corporate economy and their own
local work.

Thus far, I know, my remarks are apt to be dismissed as mere sentimentality or nostalgia, a doomed and hopeless protest against inevitable change.
And so here I must interject a pair of questions that agricultural economists
and other hardheaded realists are inclined to overlook:

First, what if all change is *not* inevitable? What if we have a choice? I am
aware that determinists and predestinarians of various sorts have argued
that we have no choice, no freedom of will, at all. I am also aware that many
people in the mainstream of our tradition have argued the opposite. It may
not be possible to settle this difference by means of proofs. But we ought at
least to remember that our idea of human dignity and worth rests upon the
assumption that we have real choices to make and that we are, because of
that, responsible for ourselves. We should remember too that implicit in
the possibility of real choice is the possibility of choosing wrong.

The second question, therefore, is: What if we've been wrong? What if
farmers, farm families, and farm communities are not expendable "extras" in
the drama of industrial progress, but instead are indispensable to the health
and the long-term survival of our food supply? What if good farmers belong
inalienably to the "land resource," and that without them the resource will

inevitably decline in productivity? What then? Well, then, we must hope to think and work our way to a better result than mere circumstance can bring us to. And although the farm population has been generally regarded for half a century as expendable, we must remember that we have *no* evidence that this is true, and much evidence that it is not.

Kentucky, until now, or until recently, has been somewhat an exception to the rule. Our farmers and rural communities have survived somewhat better than those in other places, thanks to tobacco and to the production control and price supports of the tobacco program. And it is largely because of the intensifying threat to tobacco that Kentucky has become exceptional in another way: Kentucky farmers and their allies have moved quickly to protect and enliven their local economies by diversification and local marketing. They are working to shift their dependency from the global tobacco economy to the local food economy.

One of the most promising recent developments is the awakening of some of our urban neighbors to our plight. Those of us who have been involved in various efforts to strengthen our state's rural economy have been much encouraged by offerings of support and friendship from urban consumers, business leaders, and public officials, from individual physicians and from medical organizations, from some churches, from some grocery stores, restaurants, and chefs. Efforts to preserve our rural landscapes and rural communities have received sympathetic attention from some of the states' newspaper writers. All of these people are acknowledging that there are not two separate fates, urban and rural, but ultimately only one fate that is shared. Ultimately, a city cannot be better than its surrounding countryside, and vice versa.

The recent history of agriculture in Kentucky has thus produced an outline of hope for a revival of the principle of local economy. I admit that I am astonished to have seen this happen so quickly. Because of these various efforts, it is becoming possible to imagine a return of solvency and good maintenance to our small farms, and of prosperity and paint to our country towns.

But now, having confessed to so much gratification, I must remind you that the word I used was "hope." At present, we are a long way from celebration, let alone optimism. We had better not forget that when we talk about farming we are talking about a rural economy that has been depressed for a long time. In our country, neither the land nor the people of the land ever have been valued as they should have been. The American food system—from the suppliers of agricultural technology to the chain stores—has been extremely lucrative to everybody but the people who have produced the food. For decades now we have watched great corporations and food conglomerates grow rich and powerful on the work of struggling and failing farmers, and we have heard supposed friends of agriculture hail this as "progress." We know that neither these great industries nor most of our national politicians can be expected to look kindly upon decent prices to farmers for their products.

We know too that immense fortunes and innumerable careers have been invested in the idea that agriculture is an industry and therefore subject to the same uniformity as a factory—the same large-scale techniques and technologies, the same Holstein cow and Suffolk sheep, the same crops, everywhere.

There is also the problem of the still-declining farm population. And here we need answers that only time can give. Can so steep and rapid a population decline be stopped or reversed? Can we keep a significant number of farm-bred children on the farm? Can we attract (and adequately educate) anybody else? Such questions lead us inescapably to the recognition that in the United States—and apparently in all "developed" and "developing" countries—farmers are an oppressed social class. They see that they are not only poorly paid for their work, but also ridiculed, caricatured, stereotyped, and sometimes explicitly hated by people in the media and by the public at large. Like other oppressed classes, farm people too often apply the judgment of society to themselves. Too many times I have heard an intelligent, knowledgeable, courageous, and likeable person say, "I'm just a farmer."

It is fair, I think, and even necessary to say that rural Kentucky is not the place for optimism. Our agricultural problems, at this point, are bigger and better established than any of the established solutions. If we want our rural economy to survive, we must recognize that we have a long job of work ahead of us. We must recognize, moreover, that our rural economy can survive only by becoming better than it has ever been, more skillful at meeting the needs of both the land and the people.

What, then, can we do? This is a question that is sometimes asked as a prelude to doing nothing. But the mercy of our situation is that there *are* things that can be done. A further mercy is that these are interesting and even fascinating things. I am going to list some of the things that have occurred to me, asking you to bear in mind that this is *my* list, my way of going to work, and I know that everybody goes to work a little differently.

We need to recognize better than we do the specific requirements imposed by topography, soil type, history, and all the other considerations that make up the nature of a place, and that make each place different from every other place. This is especially important where the landscapes are hilly and vulnerable to erosion.

Such a landscape also requires us to address the issue of scale. In general, the more irregular and sloping a landscape is, the more care it requires, and the better it is to use it in small parcels. The rolling uplands of Kentucky, for example, cannot be farmed like central Illinois without severe penalties. In our efforts to increase income from our fields and woodlands, there is no necessary dependence on largeness of scale, either in farming and forestry or in value-adding industries.

We need to find better ways to understand and to talk about the worth of such supposedly unquantifiable "values" as community stability or community health. It is by now undeniable that we have been wrong in assuming that we may safely wreck our rural communities for the improvement of urban communities. What we can see now, in fact, is that the willingness to damage some communities damages all communities.

We need to do everything we can to encourage urban concern for the fate of the countryside and the country people. We would benefit in innumerable ways from a system of economic alliances between local producers and local consumers. As I have mentioned, this work of developing local land-based economies has already begun. It will be hastened and strengthened, I believe, by the realization that the global economy is no longer merely a threat to our rural producers, but is already destroying our rural producers. And the only conceivable defense against the workings of the global economy, which is indifferent to all localities, is a system of healthy local economies.

We have tended to think of the rural economy as a rather loose assemblage of separate enterprises. Now we need to learn to think of it as at least potentially a single diverse but coherent system, not only of the production of rural goods, but also of ecological and community relations, all mutually healthful and necessary.

In trying to deal with our rural problems, all of us are bound to be troubled by our need to learn more and to teach more. Common sense tells us—and our experience shows us—that economy and ecology are ultimately the same, just as economy and community are ultimately the same; ultimately, people cannot expect to prosper by doing damage to the land and to human communities. A lot of us could now agree to that general statement. The problem is that at this point none of us can be very confident of knowing what that statement implies, or what it might eventually lead us to in practice. There is a great need now to learn what *works*, and not in terms just of production or agronomy or technology or technique. We need to know what works to protect the health of farms and farm families, and the health of the ecosystems and watersheds where farming is done, and the health of the consumers and users of the products of farming. We need to know what works to lift a farm family out of debt and onto its feet. We need to know what works to put locally owned businesses back in rural towns and to keep money circulating in rural communities. We need to see the accounting on what works. For the only sure way to preserve rural land is to have a thriving rural economy *on* the land.

Of all our needs none is greater or more urgent than that of encouraging farm-raised children to become farmers. For generations now a large percentage of farmers' children have been raised for export. Much the same can be said of the children of business and professional people in our country towns. We must learn to look on this as a problem, and try to find solutions. If we want our rural economy to survive, we must learn to educate our children, as Wes Jackson has said, not for "upward mobility" but for homecoming. We must not depend on the school system for this. The school system educates for export.

I believe I have just described what is necessarily our highest goal: to make rural Kentucky a place that our children and grandchildren will want to come home to. But we know that this is no simple matter. To solve this problem requires the solution of many more.

We must, for instance, begin to apply our thoughts and efforts *now* to the immense problems of medical care and health insurance. I have no statistics on this subject, but my impression is that nothing has been more effective in driving farm people off the farm than the outlandish costs of doctors, medicines, hospitals, and insurance.

That is one example of a problem that country people can't solve by themselves, as families or even as local communities. Such a problem requires them to cooperate both with one another and with their urban neighbors.

The same goes for the local marketing of local products. This idea espe-cially has been important to me; it has been like getting a better pair of glasses. Once you begin to think about the possibilities of a local economy, then you begin to see how rural and urban people, producers and consumers, could be united by local ties that would be mutually beneficial and mutu-ally pleasing, not just economic but friendly. The stakes here are extremely high. Surely the day is not far off when a lot of people will see that it is not only wrong but dangerous to permit our food supply and our health to be gathered completely into the hands of a few national and global corpora-tions while local farmers and locally owned shops, stores, and restaurants dwindle away.

We need to think always more seriously and cooperatively about the urgent need for locally owned, appropriately scaled value-adding industries situated in the countryside. So long as our rural communities are limited to the production of raw materials for export, they will bear the burdens that colonial people have always borne. We need small food-processing and woodworking plants of all kinds, both to serve directly the local communi-ties and to capture for those communities a larger share of the income from local products. We need to find ways to promote local investment in such local enterprises.

Among ourselves, we country people have got to put our minds to the problems of lowering the costs of production. We have been led to believe that we could prosper by spending a lot of money on chemicals, machines, and other purchased supplies. But that has made us more dependent and vulnerable than we were before. No farm or community can survive for very long by selling everything it produces at the lowest price while buying every-thing it needs at the highest price. What do we need that we can do or grow for ourselves? What do we need to think that we can think for our-selves? What do we have or know that we can share with one another?

I have mentioned no task in which we could not use the help of our pub-lic, tax-supported institutions. I am not recommending forgetfulness of that. We should neglect no opportunity to educate and in other ways disturb the sleep of our public servants. But neither am I recommending that we should wait for them to open their eyes to rural problems. I have not mentioned a single task that we can afford not to think about and work at, on our own, now. It is not safe to assume that anybody else will work to solve our prob-lems if *we* don't.

I have considered what I might say in earnest of my own involvement and commitment. And of course there is only one thing that I can say: I am a country person, a member of a country community. Like nearly all my known forebears, I have lived a country life, on a farm, because that has been the life I was taught to love, and it has been the life I have desired and chosen. Both of my children and their families are farming. I have five grandchildren who are growing up on farms.

You will understand that I am bragging when I say that my children are farmers. But you will not be surprised when I say also that I have worried my share over the thought that partly because of my influence, my love of farming, my children have retained their membership in a population which, if it were not human, would be said to be "endangered." And yet I am proud of them, and am profoundly grateful for their choice.

Last summer my granddaughter, Virginia, who was eleven, put in some long days on the tobacco setter. She was good at it, and all of us are pleased with her. She told her mother: "What is good about hard work is that it teaches you about little pleasures." She said that when the weather was hot and a little breeze came, it made her happy and she was grateful. I think this is something very important to know. I hope that, when the time comes, this knowledge of little pleasures will preserve her from the common assumption that pleasures have to be big, expensive, and dangerous. I am thankful that she could learn this in the same way that her parents and grandparents learned it. I am thankful that we have continued so far.

I hope it will be possible for my great-grandchildren to learn the same thing that Virginia learned, by working with their parents in the same homeland. I began my own defense of that possibility more than thirty years ago, when I had far fewer allies than I have now. For me, it is a long time too late to quit.

(1997)

Two Minds

HUMAN ORDERS—scientific, artistic, social, economic, and political—
are fictions. They are untrue, not because they necessarily are false, but
because they necessarily are incomplete. All of our human orders, however
inclusive we may try to make them, turn out to be to some degree exclusive.
And so we are always being surprised by something we find, too late, that
we have excluded. Think of almost any political revolution or freedom
movement or the ozone hole or mad cow disease or the events of September 11, 2001.

The present order, thus surprised, is then required to accommodate new
knowledge and thus to be reordered. Thomas Kuhn described this process
in *The Structure of Scientific Revolutions*.

But these surprises and changes obviously have their effect also on individual lives and on whole cultures. All of our fictions labor under an ever-
failing need to be true. And this means that they labor under an obligation
to be continuously revised.

Or, to put it another way, we humans necessarily make pictures in our
minds of our places and our world. But we can do this only by selection, putting some things into the picture and leaving the rest out. And so we live
in two landscapes, one superimposed upon the other.

First there is the cultural landscape made up of our own knowledge of
where we are, of landmarks and memories, of patterns of use and travel, of
remindings and meanings. The cultural landscape, among other things, is a
pattern of exchanges of work, goods, and comforts among neighbors. It is
the country we have in mind.

And then there is the actual landscape, which we can never fully know,
which is always going to be to some degree a mystery, from time to time surprising us. These two landscapes are necessarily and irremediably different
from each other. But there is danger in their difference; they can become *too*

different. If the cultural landscape becomes too different from the actual landscape, then we will make practical errors that will be destructive of the actual landscape or of ourselves or of both.

You can learn this from the study of any landscape that is inhabited by humans, or from teachers such as Barry Lopez and Gary Nabhan, who have written on the traditional economies of the Arctic and the American Southwest. It is easier to understand, perhaps, when thinking about extreme landscapes: If the cultural landscapes come to be too much at odds with the actual landscapes of the Arctic or the desert, the penalties are apt to be swift and lethal. In more forgiving landscapes they will (perhaps) be slower, but finally just as dangerous.

In some temperate and well-watered areas, we humans have applied the most extreme industrial methods of landscape destruction. By disregarding the cultural landscape, and all values and protections that accrue therefrom to the actual landscape, the strip miners entirely destroy the actual landscape. Cropland erosion, caused by a serious incongruity between the cultural and the actual landscapes, is a slower form of destruction than strip mining, but given enough time, it too can be entirely destructive.

At present, in the United States and in much of the rest of the world, most of the cultural landscapes that still exist are hodgepodges of failing local memories, money-making schemes, ignorant plans, bucolic fantasies, misinformation, and the random facts that we now call "information." This is compounded by the outright destruction of innumerable burial sites and other sacred places, of natural and historical landmarks, and of entire actual landscapes. Moreover, we have enormous and increasing numbers of people who have no home landscape, though in every one of their economic acts they are affecting the actual landscapes of the world, mostly for the worse. This is a situation unprecedentedly disorderly and dangerous.

To be disconnected from any actual landscape is to be, in the practical or economic sense, without a home. To have no country carefully and practically in mind is to be without a culture. In such a situation, culture becomes purposeless and arbitrary, dividing into "popular culture," determined by commerce, advertising, and fashion, and "high culture," which is either social affectation, displaced cultural memory, or the merely aesthetic pursuits of artists and art lovers.

We are thus involved in a kind of lostness in which most people are participating more or less unconsciously in the destruction of the natural world, which is to say, the sources of their own lives. They are doing this unconsciously because they see or do very little of the actual destruction themselves, and they don't know, because they have no way to learn, how they are involved. At the same time, many of the same people fear and mourn the destruction, which they can't stop because they have no practical understanding of its causes.

Conservationists, scientists, philosophers, and others are telling us daily and hourly that our species is now behaving with colossal irrationality and that we had better become more rational. I agree as to the dimensions and danger of our irrationality. As to the possibility of curing it by rationality, or at least by the rationality of the rationalists, I have some doubts.

The trouble is not just in the way we are thinking; it is also in the way we, or anyhow we in the affluent parts of the world, are living. And it is going to be hard to define anybody's living as a series of simple choices between irrationality and rationality. Moreover, this is supposedly an age of reason; we are encouraged to believe that the governments and corporations of the affluent parts of the world are run by rational people using rational processes to make rational decisions. The dominant faith of the world in our time is in rationality. That in an age of reason, the human race, or the most wealthy and powerful parts of it, should be behaving with colossal irrationality ought to make us wonder if reason alone can lead us to do what is right.

It is often proposed, nowadays, that if we would only get rid of religion and other leftovers from our primitive past and become enlightened by scientific rationalism, we could invent the new values and ethics that are needed to preserve the natural world. This proposal is perfectly reasonable, and perfectly doubtful. It supposes that we can empirically know and rationally understand everything involved, which is exactly the supposition that has underwritten our transgressions against the natural world in the first place.

Obviously we need to use our intelligence. But how much intelligence have we got? And what sort of intelligence is it that we have? And how, at its best, does human intelligence work? In order to try to answer these questions I am going to suppose for a while that there are two different kinds of human mind: the Rational Mind and another, which, for want of a better term, I will call the Sympathetic Mind. I will say now, and try to keep myself reminded, that these terms are going to appear to be allegorical, too neat and too separate—though I need to say also that their separation was not invented by me.

The Rational Mind, without being anywhere perfectly embodied, is the mind all of us are supposed to be trying to have. It is the mind that the most powerful and influential people *think* they have. Our schools exist mainly to educate and propagate and authorize the Rational Mind. The Rational Mind is objective, analytical, and empirical; it makes itself up only by considering facts; it pursues truth by experimentation; it is uncorrupted by preconception, received authority, religious belief, or feeling. Its ideal products are the proven fact, the accurate prediction, and the "informed decision." It is, you might say, the official mind of science, industry, and government.

The Sympathetic Mind differs from the Rational Mind, not by being unreasonable, but by refusing to limit knowledge or reality to the scope of reason or factuality or experimentation, and by making reason the servant of things it considers precedent and higher.

The Rational Mind is motivated by the fear of being misled, of being wrong. Its purpose is to exclude everything that cannot empirically or experimentally be proven to be a fact.

The Sympathetic Mind is motivated by fear of error of a very different kind: the error of carelessness, of being unloving. Its purpose is to be considerate of whatever is present, to leave nothing out.

The Rational Mind is exclusive; the Sympathetic Mind, however failingly, wishes to be inclusive.

These two types certainly don't exhaust the taxonomy of minds. They are merely the two that the intellectual fashions of our age have most deliberately separated and thrown into opposition.

My purpose here is to argue in defense of the Sympathetic Mind. But my objection is not to the use of reason or to reasonability. I am objecting to the exclusiveness of the Rational Mind, which has limited itself to a selection of mental functions such as the empirical methodologies of analysis and experimentation and the attitudes of objectivity and realism. In order to go into business on its own, it has in effect withdrawn from all of human life that involves feeling, affection, familiarity, reverence, faith, and loyalty. The separability of the Rational Mind is not only the dominant fiction but also the master superstition of the modern age.

The Sympathetic Mind is under the influence of certain inborn or at least fundamental likes and dislikes. Its impulse is toward wholeness. It is moved by affection for its home place, the local topography, the local memories, and the local creatures. It hates estrangement, dismemberment, and disfigurement. The Rational Mind tolerates all these things "in pursuit of truth" or in pursuit of money—which, in modern practice, have become nearly the same pursuit.

I am objecting to the failure of the rationalist enterprise of "objective science" or "pure science" or "the disinterested pursuit of truth" to prevent massive damage both to nature and to human economy. The Rational Mind does not confess its complicity in the equation: knowledge = power = money = damage. Even so, the alliance of academic science, government, and the corporate economy, and their unifying pattern of sanctions and rewards, is obvious enough. We have resisted, so far, a state religion, but we are in danger of having both a corporate state and a state science, which some people, in both the sciences and the arts, would like to establish as a state religion.

The Rational Mind is the lowest common denominator of the government–corporation–university axis. It is the fiction that makes high intellectual ability the unquestioning servant of bad work and bad law.

Under the reign of the Rational Mind, there is no firewall between contemporary science and contemporary industry or economic development. It is entirely imaginable, for instance, that a young person might go into biology because of love for plants and animals. But such a young person had better be careful, for there is nothing to prevent knowledge gained for love of the creatures from being used to destroy them for the love of money.

Now some biologists, who have striven all their lives to embody perfectly the Rational Mind, have become concerned, even passionately concerned, about the loss of "biological diversity," and they are determined to do something about it. This is usually presented as a merely logical development from ignorance to realization to action. But so far it is only comedy. The Rational

Mind, which has been destroying biological diversity by "figuring out" some things, now proposes to save what is left of biological diversity by "figuring out" some more things. It does what it has always done before: It defines the problem as a big problem calling for a big solution; it calls in the world-class experts; it invokes science, technology, and large grants of money; it propagandizes and organizes and "gears up for a major effort." The comedy here is in the failure of these rationalists to see that as soon as they have become passionately concerned they have stepped outside the dry, objective, geometrical territory claimed by the Rational Mind, and have entered the still mysterious homeland of the Sympathetic Mind, watered by unpredictable rains and by real sweat and real tears.

The Sympathetic Mind would not forget that so-called environmental problems have causes that are in part political and therefore have remedies that are in part political. But it would not try to solve these problems merely by large-scale political protections of "the environment." It knows that they must be solved ultimately by correcting the way people use their home places and local landscapes. Politically, but also by local economic improvements, it would stop colonialism in all its forms, domestic and foreign, corporate and governmental. Its first political principle is that landscapes should not be used by people who do not live in them and share their fate. If that principle were strictly applied, we would have far less need for the principle of "environmental protection."

The Sympathetic Mind understands the vital importance of the cultural landscape. The Rational Mind, by contrast, honors no cultural landscape, and therefore has no protective loyalty or affection for any actual landscape.

The definitive practical aim of the Sympathetic Mind is to adapt local economies to local landscapes. This is necessarily the work of local cultures. It cannot be done as a world-scale *feat* of science, industry, and government. This will seem a bitter bite to the optimists of scientific rationalism, which is scornful of limits and proud of its usurpations. But the science of the Sympathetic Mind is occupied precisely with the study of limits, both natural and human.

The Rational Mind does not work from any sense of geographical whereabouts or social connection or from any basis in cultural tradition or principle or character. It does not see itself as existing or working within a context. The Rational Mind doesn't think there is a context until it gets there. Its principle is to be "objective"—which is to say, unremembering and disloyal. It works within narrow mental boundaries that it draws for itself, as directed by the requirements of its profession or academic specialty or its ambition or its desire for power or profit, thus allowing for the "trade-off" and the "externalization" of costs and effects. Even when working outdoors, it is an indoor mind.

The Sympathetic Mind, even when working indoors, is an outdoor mind. It lives within an abounding and unbounded reality, always partly mysterious, in which everything matters, in which we humans are therefore returned to our ancient need for thanksgiving, prayer, and propitiation, in which we meet again and again the ancient question: How does one become worthy to use what must be used?

Whereas the Rational Mind is the mind of analysis, explanation, and manipulation, the Sympathetic Mind is the mind of our creatureliness.

Creatureliness denotes what Wallace Stevens called "the instinctive integrations which are the reasons for living." In our creatureliness we forget the little or much that we know about the optic nerve and the light-sensitive cell, and *we see;* we forget whatever we know about the physiology of the brain, and *we think;* we forget what we know of anatomy, the nervous system, the gastrointestinal tract, and *we work, eat, and sleep.* We forget the theories and therapies of "human relationships," and we merely love the people we love, and even try to love the others. If we have any sense, we forget the fashionable determinisms, and we tell our children, "Be good. Be careful. Mind your manners. Be kind."

The Sympathetic Mind leaves the world whole, or it attempts always to do so. It looks upon people and other creatures as whole beings. It does not parcel them out into functions and uses.

The Rational Mind, by contrast, has rested its work for a long time on the proposition that all creatures are machines. This works as a sort of strainer to eliminate impurities such as affection, familiarity, and loyalty from the pursuit of knowledge, power, and profit. This machine-system assures the objectivity of the Rational Mind, which is itself understood as a machine, but it fails to account for a number of things, including the Rational Mind's own worries and enthusiasms. Why should a machine be bothered by the extinction of other machines? Would even an "intelligent" computer grieve over the disappearance of the Carolina parakeet?

The Rational Mind is preoccupied with the search for a sure way to avoid risk, loss, and suffering. For the Rational Mind, experience is likely to consist of a sequence of bad surprises and therefore must be booked as a "loss." That is why, to rationalists, the past and the present are so readily expendable or destructible in favor of the future, the era of no loss.

But the Sympathetic Mind accepts loss and suffering as the price, willingly paid, of its sympathy and affection—its wholeness.

The Rational Mind attempts endlessly to inform itself against its ruin by facts, experiments, projections, scoutings of "alternatives," hedgings against the unknown.

The Sympathetic Mind is informed by experience, by tradition-borne stories of the experiences of others, by familiarity, by compassion, by commitment, by faith.

The Sympathetic Mind is preeminently a faithful mind, taking knowingly and willingly the risks required by faith. The Rational Mind, ever in need of certainty, is always in doubt, always looking for a better way, asking, testing, disbelieving in everything but its own sufficiency to its own needs, which its experience and its own methods continually disprove. It is a skeptical, fearful, suspicious mind, and always a disappointed one, awaiting the supreme truth or discovery it expects of itself, which of itself it cannot provide.

To show how these two minds work, let us place them within the dilemma of a familiar story. Here is the parable of the lost sheep from the Gospel of St. Matthew: "If a man have an hundred sheep, and one of them be gone astray, doth he not leave the ninety and nine, and goeth into the mountains, and seeketh that which is gone astray? And if so be that he find it, verily I say unto you, he rejoiceth more of that sheep, than of the ninety and nine which went not astray."

This parable is the product of an eminently sympathetic mind, but for the moment that need not distract us. The dilemma is practical enough, and we can see readily how the two kinds of mind would deal with it.

The rationalist, we may be sure, has a hundred sheep because he has a plan for that many. The one who has gone astray has escaped not only from the flock but also from the plan. That this particular sheep should stray off in this particular place at this particular time, though it is perfectly in keeping with the nature of sheep and the nature of the world, is not at all in keeping with a rational plan. What is to be done? Well, it certainly would not be rational to leave the ninety and nine, exposed as they would then be to further whims of nature, in order to search for the one. Wouldn't it be best to consider the lost sheep a "trade-off" for the safety of the ninety-nine? Having thus agreed to his loss, the doctrinaire rationalist would then work his way through a series of reasonable questions. What would be an "acceptable risk"? What would be an "acceptable loss"? Would it not be good to do some experiments to determine how often sheep may be expected to get lost? If one sheep is likely to get lost every so often, then would it not be better to have perhaps 110 sheep? Or should one insure the flock against such expectable losses? The annual insurance premium would equal the market value of how many sheep? What is likely to be the cost of the labor of looking for one lost sheep after quitting time? How much time spent looking would equal the market value of the lost sheep? Should not one think of splicing a few firefly genes into one's sheep so that strayed sheep would glow in the dark? And so on.

But (leaving aside the theological import of the parable) the shepherd is a shepherd because he embodies the Sympathetic Mind. Because he is a man of sympathy, a man devoted to the care of sheep, a man who knows the nature of sheep and of the world, the shepherd of the parable is not surprised or baffled by his problem. He does not hang back to argue over risks, trade-offs, actuarial data, or market values. He does not quibble over fractions. He goes without hesitating to hunt for the lost sheep because he has committed himself to the care of the whole hundred, because he understands his work as the fulfillment of his whole trust, because he loves the sheep, and because he knows or imagines what it is to be lost. He does what he does on behalf of the whole flock because he wants to preserve himself as a whole shepherd.

He also does what he does because he has a particular affection for that particular sheep. To the Rational Mind, all sheep are the same; any one is the same as any other. They are interchangeable, like coins or clones or machine parts or members of "the work force." To the Sympathetic Mind, each one is different from every other. Each one is an individual whose value is never entirely reducible to market value.

The Rational Mind can and will rationalize any trade-off. The Sympathetic Mind can rationalize none. Thus we have not only the parable of the ninety and nine, but also the Buddhist vow to save all sentient beings. The parable and the vow are utterly alien to the rationalism of modern science, politics, and industry. To the Rational Mind, they "don't make sense" because they deal with hardship and risk merely by acknowledgment and acceptance. Their very point is to require a human being's suffering to involve itself in the suffering of other creatures, including that of other human beings.

The Rational Mind conceives of itself as eminently practical, and is given to boasting about its competence in dealing with "reality." But if you want to hire somebody to take care of your hundred sheep, I think you had better look past the "animal scientist" and hire the shepherd of the parable, if you can still find him anywhere. For it will continue to be more reasonable, from the point of view of the Rational Mind, to trade off the lost sheep for the sake of the sheep you have left—until only one is left.

If you think I have allowed my argument to carry me entirely into fantasy and irrelevance, then let me quote an up-to-date story that follows pretty closely the outline of Christ's parable. This is from an article by Bernard E. Rollin in *Christian Century,* December 19–26, 2001, p. 26:

> A young man was working for a company that operated a large, total-confinement swine farm. One day he detected symptoms of a disease among some of the feeder pigs. As a teen, he had raised pigs himself . . . so he knew how to treat the animals. But the company's policy was to kill any diseased animals with a blow to the head—the profit margin was considered too low to allow for treatment of individual animals. So the employee decided to come in on his own time, with his own medicine, and he cured the animals. The management's response was to fire him on the spot for violating company policy.

The young worker in the hog factory is a direct cultural descendant of the shepherd in the parable, just about opposite and perhaps incomprehensible to the "practical" rationalist. But the practical implications are still the same. Would you rather have your pigs cared for by a young man who had compassion for them or by one who would indifferently knock them in the head? Which of the two would be most likely to prevent the disease in the first place? Compassion, of course, is the crux of the issue. For "company policy" must exclude compassion; if compassion were to be admitted to consideration, such a "farm" could not exist. And yet one imagines that even the hardheaded realists of "management" must occasionally violate company policy by wondering at night what they would do if *all* the pigs got sick. (I suppose they would kill them all, collect the insurance, and move on. Perhaps all that has been foreseen and prepared for in the business plan, and there is no need, after all, to lie awake and worry.)

But what of the compassionate young man? The next sentence of Mr. Rollin's account says: "Soon the young man left agriculture for good. . ." We need to pause here to try to understand the significance of his departure.

Like a strip mine, a hog factory exists in utter indifference to the landscape. Its purpose, as an animal *factory,* is to exclude from consideration both the nature of the place where it is and the nature of hogs. That it is a factory means that it could be in *any* place, and that the hog is a "unit of production." But the young man evidently was farm-raised. He evidently had in his mind at least the memory of an actual place and at least the remnants of its cultural landscape. In that landscape, things were respected according to their nature, which made compassion possible when their nature was violated. That this young man was fired from his job for showing compassion is strictly logical, for the explicit purpose of the hog factory is to violate nature. And then, logically enough, the young man "left agriculture for good." But when you exclude compassion from agriculture, what have you done? Have you not removed something ultimately of the greatest practical worth? I believe so. But this is one of the Rational Mind's world-scale experiments that has not yet been completed.

The Sympathetic Mind is a freedom-loving mind because it knows, given the inevitable discrepancies between the cultural and the actual landscapes, that everybody involved must be free to change. The idea that science and industry and government can discover for the rest of us the ultimate truths of nature and human nature, which then can be infallibly used to regulate our life, is wrong. The true work of the sciences and the arts is to keep all of us moving, in our own lives in our own places, between the cultural and the actual landscapes, making the always necessary and the forever unfinished corrections.

When the Rational Mind establishes a "farm," the result is bad farming. There is a remarkable difference between a hog factory, which exists only for the sake of its economic product, and a good farm, which exists for many reasons, including the pleasure of the farm family, their affection for their home, their satisfaction in their good work—in short, their patriotism. Such a farm yields its economic product as a sort of side effect of the health of a flourishing place in which things live according to their nature. The hog factory attempts to be a totally rational, which is to say a totally economic, enterprise. It strips away from animal life and human work every purpose, every benefit too, that is not economic. It comes about as the result of a long effort on the part of "scientific agriculture" to remove the Sympathetic Mind from all agricultural landscapes and replace it with the Rational Mind. And so good-bye to the shepherd of the parable, and to compassionate young men who leave agriculture for good. Good-bye to the cultural landscape. Good-bye to the actual landscape. These have all been dispensed with by the Rational Mind, to be replaced by a totalitarian economy with its neat, logical concepts of world-as-factory and life-as-commodity. This is an economy excluding all decisions but "informed decisions," purporting to reduce the possibility of loss.

Nothing so entices and burdens the Rational Mind as its need, and its self-imposed responsibility, to make "informed decisions." It is certainly possible for a mind to be informed—in several ways, too. And it is certainly possible for an informed mind to make decisions on the basis of all that has informed it. But that such decisions are "informed decisions"—in the sense that "informed decisions" are predictably right, or even that they are reliably better than uninformed decisions—is open to doubt.

The ideal of the "informed decision" forces "decision makers" into a thicket of facts, figures, studies, tests, and "projections." It requires long and uneasy pondering of "cost-benefit ratios"—the costs and benefits, often, of abominations. The problem is that decisions all have to do with the future, and all the actual knowledge we have is of the past. It is impossible to make a decision, however well-informed it may be, that is assuredly right, because it is impossible to know what will happen. It is only possible to know or guess that some things *may* happen, and many things that have happened have not been foreseen.

Moreover, having made an "informed decision," even one that turns out well, there is no way absolutely to determine whether or not it was a better decision than another decision that one might have made instead. It is not possible to compare a decision that one made with a decision that one did not make. There are no "controls," no "replication plots," in experience.

The Rational Mind is under relentless pressure to justify governmental and corporate acts on an ever-increasing scale of power, extent, and influence. Given that pressure, it may be not so very surprising that the Rational Mind should have a remarkable tendency toward superstition. Reaching their mental limits, which, as humans, they must do soon enough, the rationalists begin to base their thinking on principles that are sometimes astonishingly unsound: "Creatures are machines" or "Knowledge is good" or "Growth is good" or "Science will find the answer" or "A rising tide lifts all boats." Or they approach the future with a stupefying array of computers, models, statistics, projections, calculations, cost-benefit analyses, experts, and even better computers—which of course cannot foretell the end of a horse race any better than Bertie Wooster.

And so the great weakness of the Rational Mind, contrary to its protestations, is a sort of carelessness or abandonment that takes the form of high-stakes gambling—as when, with optimism and fanfare, without foreknowledge or self-doubt or caution, nuclear physicists or chemists or genetic engineers release their products into the whole world, making the whole world their laboratory.

Or the great innovators and decision makers build huge airplanes whose loads of fuel make them, in effect, flying bombs. And they build the World Trade Center, forgetting apparently the B-25 bomber that crashed into the seventy-ninth floor of the Empire State Building in 1945. And then on September 11, 2001, some enemies—of a kind we well knew we had and evidently had decided to ignore—captured two huge airplanes and flew them, as bombs, into the two towers of the World Trade Center. In retrospect, we may doubt that these shaping decisions were properly informed, just as we may doubt that the expensive "intelligence" that is supposed to foresee and prevent such disasters is sufficiently intelligent.

The decisions, if the great innovators and decision makers were given to reading poetry, might have been informed by James Laughlin's poem "Above the City," which was written soon after the B-25 crashed into the Empire State Building:

You know our office on the 18th
floor of the Salmon Tower looks
right out on the

Empire State & it just happened
we were finishing up some
late invoices on

a new book that Saturday morning
when a bomber roared through the
mist and crashed

flames poured from the windows
into the drifting clouds & sirens
screamed down in

the streets below it was unearthly
but you know the strangest thing
we realized that

none of us were much surprised because we'd always known that those
two Paragons of

Progress sooner or later would perform before our eyes this demon-
stration of their
true relationship

It is tempting now to call this poem "prophetic." But it is so only in the sense that it is insightful; it perceives the implicit contradiction between tall buildings and airplanes. This contradiction was readily apparent also to the terrorists of September 11, but evidently invisible within the mist of technological euphoria that had surrounded the great innovators and decision makers.

In the several dimensions of its horror the destruction of the World Trade Center exceeds imagination, and that tells us something. But as a physical event it is as comprehensible as 1 + 1, and that tells us something else.

Now that terrorism has established itself among us as an inescapable consideration, even the great decision makers are beginning to see that we are surrounded by the results of great decisions not adequately informed. We have built many nuclear power plants, each one a potential catastrophe, that will have to be protected, not only against their inherent liabilities and dangers, but against terrorist attack. And we have made, in effect, one thing of our food supply system, and that will have to be protected (if possible) from bioterrorism. These are by no means the only examples of the way we have exposed ourselves to catastrophic harm and great expense by our informed, rational acceptance of the normalcy of bigness and centralization.

After September 11, it can no longer be believed that science, technology, and industry are only good or that they serve only one "side." That never has been more than a progressivist and commercial superstition. Any power that belongs to one side belongs, for worse as well as better, to all sides, as indifferent as the sun that rises "on the evil and on the good." Only in the narrowest view of history can the scientists who worked on the nuclear bomb be said to have worked for democracy and freedom. They worked inescapably also for the enemies of democracy and freedom. If terrorists get possession of a nuclear bomb and use it, then the scientists of the bomb will be seen to have worked also for terrorism. There is (so far as I can now see) nothing at all that the Rational Mind can do, after the fact, to make this truth less true or less frightening. This predicament cries out for a different kind of mind before and after the fact: a mind faithful and compassionate that will not rationalize about the "good use" of destructive power, but will repudiate *any* use of it.

Freedom also is neutral, of course, and serves evil as well as good. But freedom rests on the power of good—by free speech, for instance—to correct evil. A great destructive power simply prevents this small decency of freedom. There is no way to correct a nuclear explosion.

In the midst of the dangers of the Rational Mind's achievement of bigness and centralization, the Sympathetic Mind is as hard-pressed as a pacifist in the midst of a war. There is no greater violence that ends violence, and no greater bigness with which to solve the problems of bigness. All that the Sympathetic Mind can do is maintain its difference, preserve its own integrity, and attempt to see the possibility of something better.

The Sympathetic Mind, as the mind of our creatureliness, accepts life in this world for what it is: mortal, partial, fallible, complexly dependent, entailing many responsibilities toward ourselves, our places, and our fellow beings. Above all, it understands itself as limited. It knows without embarrassment its own irreducible ignorance, especially of the future. It deals with the issue of the future, not by knowing what is going to happen, but by knowing— within limits—what to expect, and what should be required, of itself, of its neighbors, and of its place. Its decisions are informed by its culture, its experience, its understanding of nature. Because it is aware of its limits and its ignorance, it is alert to issues of scale. The Sympathetic Mind knows from experience—not with the brain only, but with the body—that danger increases with height, temperature, speed, and power. It knows by common sense and instinct that the way to protect a building from being hit by an airplane is to make it shorter; that the way to keep a nuclear power plant from becoming a weapon is not to build it; that the way to increase the security of a national food supply is to increase the agricultural self-sufficiency of states, regions, and local communities.

Because it is the mind of our wholeness, our involvement with all things beyond ourselves, the Sympathetic Mind is alert as well to the issues of propriety, of the fittingness of our artifacts to their places and to our own circumstances, needs, and hopes. It is preoccupied, in other words, with the fidelity or the truthfulness of the cultural landscape to the actual landscape.

I know I am not the only one reminded by the World Trade Center of the Tower of Babel: "let us build . . . a tower, whose top may reach unto heaven; and let us make us a name, lest we be scattered abroad upon the face of the whole earth." All extremely tall buildings have made me think of the Tower of Babel, and this started a long time before September, 11, 2001, for reasons that have become much clearer to me now that "those two Paragons of / progress" have demonstrated again "their true relationship."

Like all such gigantic buildings, from Babel onward, the World Trade Center was built without reference to its own landscape or to any other. And the reason in this instance is not far to find. The World Trade Center had no reference to a landscape because world trade, as now practiced, has none. World trade now exists to exploit indifferently the landscapes of the world, and to gather the profits to centers whence they may be distributed to the world's wealthiest people. World trade needs centers precisely to prevent the world's wealth from being "scattered abroad upon the face of the whole earth." Such centers, like the "global free market" and the "global village," are utopias, "no-places." They need to be no-places, because they respect no places and are loyal to no place.

As for the problem of building on Manhattan Island, the Rational Mind has reduced that also to a simple economic principle: Land is expensive but air is cheap; therefore, build in the air. In the early 1960's my family and I lived on the Lower West Side, not far uptown from what would become the site of the World Trade Center. The area was run down, already under the judgment of "development." But once, obviously, it had been a coherent, thriving local neighborhood of residential apartments and flats, small shops and stores, where merchants and customers knew one another and neighbors were known to neighbors. Walking from our building to the Battery was a pleasant thing to do because one had the sense of being in a real place that kept both the signs of its old human history and the memory of its geographical identity. The last time I went there, the place had been utterly dis-placed by the World Trade Center.

Exactly the same feat of displacement is characteristic of the air transportation industry, which exists to free travel from all considerations of place. Air travel reduces place to space in order to traverse it in the shortest possible time. And like gigantic buildings, gigantic airports must destroy their places and become no-places in order to exist.

People of the modern world, who have accepted the dominance and the value system of the Rational Mind, do not object, it seems, to this displacement, or to the consequent disconnection of themselves from neighborhoods and from the landscapes that support them, or to their own anonymity within crowds of strangers. These things, according to cliché, free one from the suffocating intimacies of rural or small town life. And yet we now are obliged to notice that placelessness, centralization, gigantic scale, crowdedness, and anonymity are conditions virtually made to order for terrorists.

It is wrong to say, as some always do, that catastrophes are "acts of God" or divine punishments. But it is not wrong to ask if they may not be the result of our misreading of reality or our own nature, and if some correction may not be needed. My own belief is that the Rational Mind has been performing impressively within the narrowly drawn boundaries of what it provably knows, but it has been doing badly in dealing with the things of which it is ignorant: the future, the mysterious wholeness and multiplicity of the natural world, the needs of human souls, and even the real bases of the human economy in nature, skill, kindness, and trust. Increasingly, it seeks to justify itself with intellectual superstitions, public falsehoods, secrecy, and mistaken hopes, responding to its failures and bad surprises with (as the terrorists intend) terror and with ever grosser applications of power.

But the Rational Mind is caught, nevertheless, in cross-purposes that are becoming harder to ignore. It is altogether probable that there is an executive of an air-polluting industry who has a beloved child who suffers from asthma caused by air pollution. In such a situation the Sympathetic Mind cries, "Stop! Change your life! Quit your job! At least try to discover the cause of the harm and *do* something about it!" And here the Rational Mind must either give way to the Sympathetic Mind, or it must recite the conventional excuse that is a confession of its failure: "There is nothing to be done. This is the way things are. It is inevitable."

The same sort of contradiction now exists between national security and the global economy. Our government, having long ago abandoned any thought of economic self-sufficiency, having ceded a significant measure of national sovereignty to the World Trade Organization, and now terrified by terrorism, is obliged to police the global economy against the transportation of contraband weapons, which can be detected if the meshes of the surveillance network are fine enough, and also against the transportation of diseases, which cannot be detected. This too will be excused, at least for a while, by the plea of inevitability, never mind that this is the result of a conflict of policies and of "informed decisions." Meanwhile, there is probably no landscape in the world that is not threatened with abuse or destruction as a result of somebody's notion of trade or somebody's notion of security.

When the Rational Mind undertakes to work on a large scale, it works clumsily. It inevitably does damage, and it cannot exempt even itself or its own from the damage it does. You cannot help to pollute the world's only atmosphere and exempt your asthmatic child. You cannot make allies and enemies of the same people at the same time. Finally the idea of the trade-off fails. When the proposed trade-off is on the scale of the whole world— the natural world for world trade, world peace for national security—it can fail only into world disaster.

⌇

The Rational Mind, while spectacularly succeeding in some things, fails completely when it tries to deal in materialist terms with the part of reality that is spiritual. Religion and the language of religion deal approximately and awkwardly enough with this reality, but the Rational Mind, though it apparently cannot resist the attempt, cannot deal with it at all.

But most of the most important laws for the conduct of human life probably are religious in origin—laws such as these: Be merciful, be forgiving, love your neighbors, be hospitable to strangers, be kind to other creatures, take care of the helpless, love your enemies. We must, in short, love and care for one another and the other creatures. We are allowed to make no exceptions. Every person's obligation toward the Creation is summed up in two words from Genesis 2:15: "Keep it."

It is impossible, I believe, to make a neat thing of this set of instructions. It is impossible to disentangle its various obligations into a list of discrete items. Selfishness, or even "enlightened self-interest," cannot find a place to poke in its awl. One's obligation to oneself cannot be isolated from one's obligation to everything else. The whole thing is balanced on the verb *to love*. Love for oneself finds its only efficacy in love for everything else. Even loving one's enemy has become a strategy of self-love as the technology of death has grown greater. And this the terrorists have discovered and have accepted: The death of your enemy is your own death. The whole network of interdependence and obligation is a neatly set trap. Love does not let us escape from it; it turns the trap itself into the means and fact of our only freedom.

This condition of lawfulness and this set of laws did not originate in the Rational Mind, and could not have done so. The Rational Mind reduces our complex obligation to care for one another to issues of justice, forgetting the readiness with which we and our governments reduce justice, in turn, to revenge; and forgetting that even justice is intolerable without mercy, forgiveness, and love.

Justice is a rational procedure. Mercy is not a procedure and it is not rational. It is a kind of freedom that comes from sympathy, which is to say imagination—the *felt* knowledge of what it is to be another person or another creature. It is free because it does not have to be just. Justice is desirable, of course, but it is virtually the opposite of mercy. Mercy, says the Epistle of James, "rejoiceth against judgment."

As for the law requiring us to "keep" the given or the natural world (to go in search of the lost sheep, to save all sentient beings), the Rational Mind, despite the reasonable arguments made by some ecologists and biologists, cannot cover that distance either. In response to the proposition that we are responsible for the health of all the world, the Rational Mind begins to insist upon exceptions and trade-offs. It begins to designate the profit-yielding parts of the world that may "safely" be destroyed, and those unprofitable parts that may be preserved as "natural" or "wild." It divides the domestic from the wild, the human from the natural. It conceives of a natural place as a place where no humans live. Places where humans live are not natural, and the nature of such places must be reduced to comprehensibility, which is to say destroyed as they naturally are. The Rational Mind, convinced of the need to preserve "biological diversity," wants to preserve it in "nature preserves." It cannot conceive or tolerate the possibility of preserving biological diversity in the whole world, or of an economic harmony between humans and a world that by nature exceeds human comprehension.

It is because of the world's ultimately indecipherable webwork of vital connections, dependences, and obligations, and because ultimately our response to it must be loving beyond knowing, that the works of the Rational Mind are ultimately disappointing even to some rationalists.

When the Rational Mind fails not only into bewilderment but into irrationality and catastrophe, as it repeatedly does, that is because it has so isolated itself within its exclusive terms that it goes beyond its limits without knowing it.

Finally the human mind must accept the limits of sympathy, which paradoxically will enlarge it beyond the limits of rationality, but nevertheless will limit it. It must find its freedom and its satisfaction by working within its limits, on a scale much smaller than the Rational Mind will easily accept, for the Rational Mind continually longs to extend its limits by technology. But the safe competence of human work extends no further, ever, than our ability to think and love at the same time.

Obviously, we *can* work on a gigantic scale, but just as obviously we cannot foresee the gigantic catastrophes to which gigantic works are vulnerable, any more than we can foresee the natural and human consequences of such work. We can develop a global economy, but only on the conditions that it will not be loving in its effects on its human and natural sources, and that it will risk global economic collapse. We can build gigantic works of architecture too, but only with the likelihood that the gathering of the economic means to do so will generate somewhere the will to destroy what we have built.

The efficacy of a law is in the ability of people to obey it. The larger the scale of work, the smaller will be the number of people who can obey the law that we should be loving toward the world, even those places and creatures that we must use. You will see the problem if you imagine that you are one of the many, or if you *are* one of the many, who can find no work except in a destructive industry. Whether or not it is economic slavery to have no choice of jobs, it certainly is moral slavery to have no choice but to do what is wrong.

And so conservationists have not done enough when they conserve wilderness or biological diversity. They also must conserve the possibilities of peace and good work, and to do that they must help to make a good economy. To succeed, they must help to give more and more people everywhere in the world the opportunity to do work that is both a living and a loving. This, I think, cannot be accomplished by the Rational Mind. It will require the full employment of the Sympathetic Mind—*all* the little intelligence we have.

(2002)

The Prejudice Against
Country People

ON JUNE 21, 2001, Richard Lewontin, a respected Harvard scientist,
published in *The New York Review of Books* an article on genetic engineering and the controversy about it. In the latter part of his article, Mr.
Lewontin turns away from his announced premise of scientific objectivity
to attack, in a markedly personal way, the critics of industrial agriculture and
biotechnology who are trying to defend small farmers against exploitation
by global agribusiness.

He criticizes Vandana Shiva, the Indian scientist and defender of the traditional agricultures of the Third World, for her appeal to "religious morality," and calls her a "cheerleader." He speaks of some of her allies as "a bunch
of Luddites," and he says that all such people are under the influence "of a
false nostalgia for an idyllic life never experienced." He says that present
efforts to save "the independent family farmer... are a hundred years too
late, and GMOs [genetically modified organisms] are the wrong target."
One would have thought, Mr. Lewontin says wearily, that "industrial capitalism ... has become so much the basis of European and American life
that any truly popular new romantic movement against it would be inconceivable."

Mr. Lewontin is a smart man, but I don't think he understands how conventional, how utterly trite and thoughtless, is his reaction to Ms. Shiva
and other advocates of agricultural practices that are biologically sound and
economically just. Apologists for industrialism seldom feel any need to
notice their agrarian critics, but when a little dog snaps at the heels of a big
dog long enough, now and again the big dog will have to condescend. On
such occasions, the big dog *always* says what Mr. Lewontin has said in his
article: You are a bunch of Luddites; you are a bunch of romantics motivated

by nostalgia for a past that never existed; it is too late; there is no escape. The best-loved proposition is the last: Whatever happens is inevitable; it all has been determined by economics and technology.

This is not scientific objectivity or science or scholarship. It is the luxury politics of an academic islander.

The problem for Mr. Lewontin and others like him is that the faith in industrial agriculture as an eternal pillar of human society is getting harder to maintain, not because of the attacks of its opponents but because of the increasingly manifest failures of industrial agriculture itself: massive soil erosion, soil degradation, genetic impoverishment, ecological damage, pollution by toxic chemicals, pollution by animal factory wastes, depletion of aquifers, runaway subsidies, the spread of pests and diseases by the long-distance transportation of food, mad cow disease, indifferent cruelty to animals, the many human sufferings associated with agricultural depression, exploitation of "cheap" labor, the abuse of migrant workers. And now, after the catastrophe of September 11, the media have begun to notice what critics of industrial capitalism have always known: The corporate food supply is highly vulnerable to acts of biological warfare.

That these problems exist and are serious is indisputable. So why are they so little noticed by politicians of influence, by people in the media, by university scientists and intellectuals? An increasing number of people alerted to the problems will answer immediately: Because far too many of those people are far too dependent on agribusiness contributions, advertising, and grants. That is true, but another reason that needs to be considered is modern society's widespread prejudice against country people. This prejudice is not easy to explain, in view of modern society's continuing dependence upon rural sustenance, but its existence also is indisputable.

Mr. Lewontin's condescension toward country people and their problems is not an aberration either in our society or in *The New York Review of Books*. On June 29, 2000, that magazine published this sentence: "At worst, [Rebecca West] had a mind that was closed and cold, like a small town lawyer's, prizing facts but estranged from imaginative truth." And on December 20, 2001, it published this: "The Gridiron dinner, as the affair is known, drags on for about five hours, enlivened mainly by the speeches of the politicians, whose ghostwriters in recent years have consistently outdone the journalists in the sharpness and grace of their wit (leaving journalists from the provinces with a strong impulse to follow the groundhogs back into their holes)."

It is possible to imagine that some readers will ascribe my indignation at those sentences to the paranoia of an advocate for the losing side. But I would ask those readers to imagine a reputable journal nowadays that would attribute closed, cold minds to *Jewish* lawyers, or speak of *black* journalists wanting to follow the groundhogs into their holes. This, it seems to me, would pretty effectively dissipate the ha-ha.

Disparagements of farmers, of small towns, of anything identifiable as "provincial" can be found everywhere: in comic strips, TV shows, newspaper editorials, literary magazines, and so on. A few years ago, *The New Republic* affirmed the necessity of the decline of family farms in a cover article entitled "The Idiocy of Rural Life." And I remember a Kentucky high school basketball cheer that instructed the opposing team:

> Go back, go back, go back to the woods.
> Your coach is a farmer and your team's no good.

I believe it is a fact, proven by their rapidly diminishing numbers and economic power, that the world's small farmers and other "provincial" people have about the same status now as enemy civilians in wartime. They are the objects of small, "humane" consideration, but if they are damaged or destroyed "collaterally," then "we very much regret it" but they were in the way—and, by implication, not quite as human as "we" are. The industrial and corporate powers, abetted and excused by their many dependents in government and the universities, are perpetrating a sort of economic genocide—less bloody than military genocide, to be sure, but just as arrogant, foolish, and ruthless, and perhaps more effective in ridding the world of a kind of human life. The small farmers and the people of small towns are understood as occupying the bottom step of the economic stairway and deservedly falling from it because they are rural, which is to say not metropolitan or cosmopolitan, which is to say socially, intellectually, and culturally inferior to "us."

Am I trying to argue that all small farmers are superior or that they are all good farmers or that they live the "idyllic life"? I certainly am not. And that is my point. The sentimental stereotype is just as damaging as the negative one. The image of the farmer as the salt of the earth, independent son of the soil, and child of nature is a sort of lantern slide projected over the image of the farmer as simpleton, hick, or redneck. Both images serve to obliterate any concept of farming as an ancient, useful, honorable vocation, requiring admirable intelligence and skill, a complex local culture, great patience and endurance, and moral responsibilities of the gravest kind.

I am not trying to attribute any virtues or characteristics to farmers or rural people as a category. I am only saying what black people, Jews, and others have said many times before: These stereotypes don't fit. They don't work. Of course, some small-town lawyers have minds that are "closed and cold," but some, too, have minds that are open and warm. And some "provincial" journalists may be comparable to groundhogs, I suppose, though I know of none to whom that simile exactly applies, but some too are brilliant and brave and eminently useful. I am thinking, for example, of Tom and Pat Gish, publishers of *The Mountain Eagle* in Whitesburg, Kentucky, who for many decades have opposed the coal companies whenever necessary and have unflinchingly suffered the penalties, including arson. Do I think the Gishes would be intimidated by the frivolous wit of ghostwriters at the Gridiron dinner? I do not.

I have been attentive all my life to the doings of small-town lawyers and "provincial" journalists, and I could name several of both sorts who have not been admirable, but I could name several also who have been heroes among those who wish to be just. I can say, too, that, having lived both in great metropolitan centers of culture and in a small farming community, I have seen few things dumber and tackier—or more provincial—than this half-scared, half-witted urban contempt for "provinciality."

The stereotype of the farmer as rustic simpleton or uncouth redneck is, like most stereotypes, easily refuted: All you have to do is compare it with a number of real people. But the stereotype of the small farmer as obsolete human clinging to an obsolete kind of life, though equally false, is harder to deal with because it comes from a more complicated prejudice, entrenched in superstition and a kind of insanity.

The prejudice begins in the idea that work is bad, and that manual work outdoors is the worst work of all. The superstition is that since all work is bad, all "labor-saving" is good. The insanity is in the ultimately suicidal pillage of the natural world and the land-using cultures on which human society depends for its life.

The industrialization of agriculture has replaced working people with machines and chemicals. The people thus replaced have, supposedly, gone into the "better" work of offices or factories. But in all the enterprises of the industrial economy, as in industrial war, we finally reach the end of the desk jobs, the indoor work, the glamour of forcing nature to submission by push-buttons and levers, and we come to the unsheltered use of the body. Somebody, finally, must work in the mud and the snow, build and mend the pasture fences, help the calving cow.

Now, in the United States, the despised work of agriculture is done by the still-surviving and always struggling small farmers, and by many Mexican and Central American migrant laborers who live and work a half step, if that, above slavery. The work of the farmland, in other words, is now accomplished by two kinds of oppression, and most people do not notice, or if they notice they do not care. If they are invited to care, they are likely to excuse themselves by answers long available in the "public consciousness": Farmers are better off when they lose their farms. They are improved by being freed of the "mind-numbing work" of farming. Mexican migrant field hands, like Third World workers in sweatshops, are being improved by our low regard and low wages. And besides, however objectionable from the standpoint of "nostalgia," the dispossession of farmers and their replacement by machines, chemicals, and oppressed migrants is "inevitable," and it is "too late" for correction.

Such talk, it seems to me, descends pretty directly from the old pro-slavery rhetoric: Slavery was an improvement over "savagery," the slaves were happy in their promotion, slavery was sanctioned by God. The moral difference is not impressive.

But the prejudice against rural people is not merely an offense against justice and common decency. It also obscures or distorts perception of issues and problems of the greatest practical urgency. The unacknowledged question beneath the dismissal of the agrarian small farmers is this: What is the best way to farm—not anywhere or everywhere, but in every one of the Earth's fragile localities? What is the best way to farm *this* farm? In *this* ecosystem? For *this* farmer? For *this* community? For *these* consumers? For the next seven generations? In a time of terrorism? To answer those questions, we will have to go beyond our preconceptions about farmers and other "provincial" people. And we will have to give up a significant amount of scientific objectivity, too. That is because the standards required to measure the qualities of farming are not just scientific or economic or social or cultural, but all of those, employed all together.

This line of questioning finally must encounter such issues as preference, taste, and appearance. What kind of farming and what kind of food do you *like*? How should a good steak or tomato *taste*? What does a good farm or good crop look like? Is this farm landscape healthful enough? Is it beautiful enough? Are health and beauty, as applied to landscapes, synonymous?

With such questions, we leave objective science and all other specialized disciplines behind, and we come to something like an undepartmented criticism or connoisseurship that is at once communal and personal. Even though we obviously must answer our questions about farming with all the intellectual power we have, we must not fail to answer them also with affection. I mean the complex, never-completed affection for our land and our neighbors that is true patriotism.

(2001)

The Whole Horse

*This modern mind sees only half of the horse—that half which may become
a dynamo, or an automobile, or any other horsepowered machine.
If this mind had much respect for the full-dimensioned, grass-eating horse,
it would never have invented the engine which represents only half of him.
The religious mind, on the other hand, has this respect; it wants
the whole horse, and it will be satisfied with nothing less.
I should say a religious mind that requires more than a half-religion.*

—Allen Tate, "Remarks on the Southern Religion," in *I'll Take My Stand*

ONE OF THE PRIMARY RESULTS—and one of the primary needs—of
industrialism is the separation of people and places and products from
their histories. To the extent that we participate in the industrial economy,
we do not know the histories of our meals or of our habitats or of our families. This is an economy, and in fact a culture, of the one-night stand. "I had
a good time," says the industrial lover, "but don't ask me my last name." Just
so, the industrial eater says to the svelte industrial hog, "We'll be together
at breakfast. I don't want to see you before then, and I won't care to remember you afterwards."

In this condition, we have many commodities, but little satisfaction, little sense of the sufficiency of anything. The scarcity of satisfaction makes of
our many commodities, in fact, an infinite series of commodities, the new
commodities invariably promising greater satisfaction than the older ones.
And so we can say that the industrial economy's most-marketed commodity is satisfaction, and that this commodity, which is repeatedly promised,
bought, and paid for, is never delivered. On the other hand, people who
have much satisfaction do not need many commodities.

The persistent want of satisfaction is directly and complexly related to the dissociation of ourselves and all our goods from our and their histories. If things do not last, are not made to last, they can have no histories, and we who use these things can have no memories. We buy new stuff on the promise of satisfaction because we have forgot the promised satisfaction for which we bought our old stuff. One of the procedures of the industrial economy is to reduce the longevity of materials. For example, wood, which well made into buildings and furniture and well cared for can last hundreds of years, is now routinely manufactured into products that last twenty-five years. We do not cherish the memory of shoddy and transitory objects, and so we do not remember them. That is to say that we do not invest in them the lasting respect and admiration that make for satisfaction.

The problem of our dissatisfaction with all the things that we use is not correctable within the terms of the economy that produces those things. At present, it is virtually impossible for us to know the economic history or the ecological cost of the products we buy; the origins of the products are typically too distant and too scattered and the processes of trade, manufacture, transportation, and marketing too complicated. There are, moreover, too many reasons for the industrial suppliers of these products not to want their histories to be known.

When there is no reliable accounting and therefore no competent knowledge of the economic and ecological effects of our lives, we cannot live lives that are economically and ecologically responsible. This is the problem that has frustrated, and to a considerable extent undermined, the American conservation effort from the beginning. It is ultimately futile to plead and protest and lobby in favor of public ecological responsibility while, in virtually every act of our private lives, we endorse and support an economic system that is by intention, and perhaps by necessity, ecologically irresponsible.

If the industrial economy is not correctable within or by its own terms, then obviously what is required for correction is a countervailing economic idea. And the most significant weakness of the conservation movement is its failure to produce or espouse an economic idea capable of correcting the economic idea of the industrialists. Somewhere near the heart of the conservation effort as we have known it is the romantic assumption that, if we have become alienated from nature, we can become unalienated by making nature the subject of contemplation or art, ignoring the fact that we live necessarily in and from nature—ignoring, in other words, all the economic issues that are involved. Walt Whitman could say, "I think I could turn and live with animals" as if he did not know that, in fact, we do live with animals, and that the terms of our relation to them are inescapably established by our economic use of their and our world. So long as we live, we are going to be living with skylarks, nightingales, daffodils, waterfowl, streams, forests, mountains, and all the other creatures that romantic poets and artists have yearned toward. And by the way we live we will determine whether or not those creatures will live.

That this nature-romanticism of the nineteenth century ignores economic facts and relationships has not prevented it from setting the agenda for modern conservation groups. This agenda has rarely included the economics of land use, without which the conservation effort becomes almost inevitably long on sentiment and short on practicality. The giveaway is that when conservationists try to be practical they are likely to defend the "sustainable use of natural resources" with the argument that this will make the industrial economy sustainable. A further giveaway is that the longer the industrial economy lasts in its present form, the further it will demonstrate its ultimate impossibility: Every human in the world cannot, now or ever, own the whole catalogue of shoddy, high-energy industrial products, which cannot be sustainably made or used. Moreover, the longer the industrial economy lasts, the more it will eat away the possibility of a better economy.

The conservation effort has at least brought under suspicion the general relativism of our age. Anybody who has studied with care the issues of conservation knows that our acts are being measured by a real, absolute, and unyielding standard that was invented by no human. Our acts that are not in harmony with nature are inevitably and sometimes irremediably destructive. The standard exists. But having no opposing economic idea, conservationists have had great difficulty in applying the standard.

What, then, is the countervailing idea by which we might correct the industrial idea? We will not have to look hard to find it, for there is only one, and that is agrarianism. Our major difficulty (and danger) will be in attempting to deal with agrarianism as "an idea"—agrarianism is primarily a practice, a set of attitudes, a loyalty, and a passion; it is an idea only secondarily and at a remove. To use merely the handiest example: I was raised by agrarians, my bias and point of view from my earliest childhood were agrarian, and yet I never heard agrarianism defined, or even so much as named, until I was a sophomore in college. I am well aware of the danger in defining things, but if I am going to talk about agrarianism, I am going to have to define it. The definition that follows is derived both from agrarian writers, ancient and modern, and from the unliterary and sometimes illiterate agrarians who have been my teachers.

The fundamental difference between industrialism and agrarianism is this: Whereas industrialism is a way of thought based on monetary capital and technology, agrarianism is a way of thought based on land.

Agrarianism, furthermore, is a culture at the same time that it is an economy. Industrialism is an economy before it is a culture. Industrial culture is an accidental by-product of the ubiquitous effort to sell unnecessary products for more than they are worth.

An agrarian economy rises up from the fields, woods, and streams—from the complex of soils, slopes, weathers, connections, influences, and exchanges that we mean when we speak, for example, of the local community or the local watershed. The agrarian mind is therefore not regional or national, let alone global, but local. It must know on intimate terms the local plants and animals and local soils; it must know local possibilities and impossibilities, opportunities and hazards. It depends and insists on knowing very particular local histories and biographies.

Because a mind so placed meets again and again the necessity for work to be good, the agrarian mind is less interested in abstract quantities than in particular qualities. It feels threatened and sickened when it hears people and creatures and places spoken of as labor, management, capital, and raw material. It is not at all impressed by the industrial legendry of gross national products, or of the numbers sold and dollars earned by gigantic corporations. It is interested—and forever fascinated—by questions leading toward the accomplishment of good work: What is the best location for a particular building or fence? What is the best way to plow *this* field? What is the best course for a skid road in *this* woodland? Should *this* tree be cut or spared? What are the best breeds and types of livestock for *this* farm?— questions which cannot be answered in the abstract, and which yearn not toward quantity but toward elegance. Agrarianism can never become abstract because it has to be practiced in order to exist.

And though this mind is local, almost absolutely placed, little attracted to mobility either upward or lateral, it is not provincial; it is too taken up and fascinated by its work to feel inferior to any other mind in any other place.

An agrarian economy is always a subsistence economy before it is a market economy. The center of an agrarian farm is the household. The function of the household economy is to assure that the farm family lives from the farm so far as possible. It is the subsistence part of the agrarian economy that assures its stability and its survival. A subsistence economy necessarily is highly diversified, and it characteristically has involved hunting and gathering as well as farming and gardening. These activities bind people to their local landscape by close, complex interests and economic ties. The industrial economy alienates people from the native landscape precisely by breaking these direct practical ties and introducing distant dependences.

Agrarian people of the present, knowing that the land must be well cared for if anything is to last, understand the need for a settled connection, not just between farmers and their farms, but between urban people and their surrounding and tributary landscapes. Because the knowledge and know-how of good caretaking must be handed down to children, agrarians recognize the necessity of preserving the coherence of families and communities.

The stability, coherence, and longevity of human occupation require that the land should be divided among many owners and users. The central figure of agrarian thought has invariably been the small owner or small-holder who maintains a significant measure of economic self-determination on a small acreage. The scale and independence of such holdings imply two things that agrarians see as desirable: intimate care in the use of the land, and political democracy resting upon the indispensable foundation of economic democracy.

A major characteristic of the agrarian mind is a longing for independence —that is, for an appropriate degree of personal and local self-sufficiency. Agrarians wish to earn and deserve what they have. They do not wish to live by piracy, beggary, charity, or luck.

In the written record of agrarianism, there is a continually recurring affirmation of nature as the final judge, lawgiver, and pattern-maker of and for the human use of the earth. We can trace the lineage of this thought in the West through the writings of Virgil, Spenser, Shakespeare, Pope, Jefferson, and on into the work of the twentieth-century agriculturists and scientists J. Russell Smith, Liberty Hyde Bailey, Albert Howard, Wes Jackson, John Todd, and others. The idea is variously stated: We should not work until we have looked and seen where we are; we should honor Nature not only as our mother or grandmother, but as our teacher and judge; we should "let the forest judge"; we should "consult the Genius of the Place"; we should make the farming fit the farm; we should carry over into the cultivated field the diversity and coherence of the native forest or prairie. And this way of thinking is surely allied to that of the medieval scholars and architects who saw the building of a cathedral as a symbol or analogue of the creation of the world. The agrarian mind is, at bottom, a religious mind. It subscribes to Allen Tate's doctrine of "the whole horse." It prefers the Creation itself to the powers and quantities to which it can be reduced. And this is a mind completely different from that which sees creatures as machines, minds as computers, soil fertility as chemistry, or agrarianism as an idea. John Haines has written that "the eternal task of the artist and the poet, the historian and the scholar . . . is to find the means to reconcile what are two separate and yet inseparable histories, Nature and Culture. To the extent that we can do this, the 'world' makes sense to us and can be lived in." I would add only that this applies also to the farmer, the forester, the scientist, and others.

The agrarian mind begins with the love of fields and ramifies in good farming, good cooking, good eating, and gratitude to God. Exactly analogous to the agrarian mind is the sylvan mind that begins with the love of forests and ramifies in good forestry, good woodworking, good carpentry, and gratitude to God. These two kinds of mind readily intersect; neither ever intersects with the industrial-economic mind. The industrial-economic mind begins with ingratitude, and ramifies in the destruction of farms and forests. The "lowly" and "menial" arts of farm and forest are mostly taken for granted or ignored by the culture of the "fine arts" and by "spiritual" religions; they are taken for granted or ignored or held in contempt by the powers of the industrial economy. But in fact they are inescapably the foundation of human life and culture, and their adepts are capable of as deep satisfactions and as high attainments as anybody else.

Having, so to speak, laid industrialism and agrarianism side by side, implying a preference for the latter, I will be confronted by two questions that I had better go ahead and answer.

The first is whether or not agrarianism is simply a "phase" that we humans had to go through and then leave behind in order to get onto the track of technological progress toward ever greater happiness. The answer is that although industrialism has certainly conquered agrarianism, and has very nearly destroyed it altogether, it is also true that in every one of its uses of the natural world industrialism is in the process of catastrophic failure. Industry is now desperately shifting—by means of genetic engineering, global colonialism, and other contrivances—to prolong its control of our farms and forests, but the failure nonetheless continues. It is not possible to argue sanely in favor of soil erosion, water pollution, genetic impoverishment, and the destruction of rural communities and local economies. Industrialism, unchecked by the affections and concerns of agrarianism, becomes monstrous. And this is because of a weakness identified by the Twelve Southerners of *I'll Take My Stand* in their "Statement of Principles": Under the rule of industrialism "the remedies proposed . . . are always homeopathic." That is to say that industrialism always proposes to correct its errors and excesses by more industrialization.

The second question is whether or not by espousing the revival of agrarianism we will commit the famous sin of "turning back the clock." The answer to that, for present-day North Americans, is fairly simple. The overriding impulse of agrarianism is toward the local adaptation of economies and cultures. Agrarian people wish to adapt the farming to the farm and the forestry to the forest. At times and in places we latter-day Americans have come close to accomplishing this goal, and we have a few surviving examples, but it is generally true that we are much further from local adaptation now than we were fifty years ago. We never yet have developed stable, sustainable, locally adapted land-based economies. The good rural enterprises and communities that we will find in our past have been almost constantly under threat from the colonialism, first foreign and then domestic, and now "global," which has so far dominated our history, and which has been institutionalized for a long time in the industrial economy. The possibility of an authentically settled country still lies ahead of us.

If we wish to look ahead, we will see not only in the United States but in the world two economic programs that conform pretty exactly to the aims of industrialism and agrarianism as I have described them.

The first is the effort to globalize the industrial economy, not merely by the expansionist programs of supra-national corporations within themselves, but also by means of government-sponsored international trade agreements, the most prominent of which is the World Trade Organization Agreement, which institutionalizes the industrial ambition to use, sell, or destroy every acre and every creature of the world.

The World Trade Organization gives the lie to the industrialist conservatives' professed abhorrence of big government. The cause of big government, after all, is big business. The power to do large-scale damage, which is gladly assumed by every large-scale industrial enterprise, calls naturally and logically for government regulation, which of course the corporations object to. But we have a good deal of evidence also that the leaders of big business actively desire and promote big government. They and their political allies, while ostensibly working to "downsize" government, continue to promote government helps and "incentives" to large corporations; and, however absurdly, they adhere to their notion that a small government, taxing only the working people, can maintain a big highway system, a big military establishment, a big space program, and big government contracts.

But the most damaging evidence is the World Trade Organization itself, which is in effect a global government, with power to enforce the decisions of the collective against national laws that conflict with it. The coming of the World Trade Organization was foretold seventy years ago in the "Statement of Principles" of *I'll Take My Stand*, which said that "the true Sovietists or Communists . . . are the industrialists themselves. They would have the government set up an economic super-organization, which in turn would become the government." The agrarians of *I'll Take My Stand* did not foresee this because they were fortune-tellers, but because they had perceived accurately the character and motive of the industrial economy.

The second program, counter to the first, is composed of many small efforts to preserve or improve or establish local economies. These efforts on the part of nonindustrial or agrarian conservatives, local patriots, are taking place in countries both affluent and poor all over the world.

Whereas the corporate sponsors of the World Trade Organization, in order to promote their ambitions, have required only the hazy glamour of such phrases as "the global economy," "the global context," and "globalization," the local economists use a much more diverse and particularizing vocabulary that you can actually think with: "community," "ecosystem," "watershed," "place," "homeland," "family," "household."

And whereas the global economists advocate a world-government-by-economic-bureaucracy, which would destroy local adaptation everywhere by ignoring the uniqueness of every place, the local economists found their work upon respect for such uniqueness. Places differ from one another, the local economists say, therefore we must behave with unique consideration in each one; the ability to tender an appropriate practical regard and respect to each place in its difference is a kind of freedom; the inability to do so is a kind of tyranny. The global economists are the great centralizers of our time. The local economists, who have so far attracted the support of no prominent politician, are the true decentralizers and downsizers, for they seek an appropriate degree of self-determination and independence for localities. They seem to be moving toward a radical and necessary revision of our idea of a city. They are learning to see the city, not just as a built and paved municipality set apart by "city limits" to live by trade and transportation from the world at large, but rather as a part of a local community which includes also the city's rural neighbors, its surrounding landscape and its watershed, on which it might depend for at least some of its necessities, and for the health of which it might exercise a competent concern and responsibility.

At this point, I want to say point blank what I hope is already clear: Though agrarianism proposes that everybody has agrarian responsibilities, it does not propose that everybody should be a farmer or that we do not need cities. Nor does it propose that every product should be a necessity. Furthermore, any thinkable human economy would have to grant to manufacturing an appropriate and honorable place. Agrarians would insist only that any manufacturing enterprise should be formed and scaled to fit the local landscape, the local ecosystem, and the local community, and that it should be locally owned and employ local people. They would insist, in other words, that the shop or factory owner should not be an outsider, but rather a sharer in the fate of the place and its community. The deciders should have to live with the results of their decisions.

Between these two programs—the industrial and the agrarian, the global and the local—the most critical difference is that of knowledge. The global economy institutionalizes a global ignorance, in which producers and consumers cannot know or care about one another, and in which the histories of all products will be lost. In such a circumstance, the degradation of products and places, producers and consumers is inevitable.

But in a sound local economy, in which producers and consumers are neighbors, nature will become the standard of work and production. Consumers who understand their economy will not tolerate the destruction of the local soil or ecosystem or watershed as a cost of production. Only a healthy local economy can keep nature and work together in the consciousness of the community. Only such a community can restore history to economics.

I will not be altogether surprised to be told that I have set forth here a line of thought that is attractive but hopeless. A number of critics have advised me of this, out of their charity, as if I might have written of my hopes for forty years without giving a thought to hopelessness. Hope, of course, is always accompanied by the fear of hopelessness, which is a legitimate fear.

And so I would like to conclude by confronting directly the issue of hope. My hope is most seriously challenged by the fact of decline, of loss. The things that I have tried to defend are less numerous and worse off now than when I started, but in this I am only like all other conservationists. All of us have been fighting a battle that on average we are losing, and I doubt that there is any use in reviewing the statistical proofs. The point—the only interesting point—is that we have not quit. Ours is not a fight that you can stay in very long if you look on victory as a sign of triumph or on loss as a sign of defeat. We have not quit because we are not hopeless.

My own aim is not hopelessness. I am not looking for reasons to give up. I am looking for reasons to keep on. In outlining here the concerns of agrarianism, I have intended to show how the effort of conservation could be enlarged and strengthened.

What agrarian principles implicitly propose—and what I explicitly propose in advocating those principles at this time—is a revolt of local small producers and local consumers against the global industrialism of the corporations. Do I think that there is a hope that such a revolt can survive and succeed, and that it can have a significant influence upon our lives and our world?

Yes, I do. And to be as plain as possible, let me just say what I know. I know from friends and neighbors and from my own family that it is now possible for farmers to sell at a premium to local customers such products as organic vegetables, organic beef and lamb, and pasture-raised chickens. This market is being made by the exceptional goodness and freshness of the food, by the wish of urban consumers to support their farming neighbors, and by the excesses and abuses of the corporate food industry.

This is the pattern of an economic revolt that is not only possible but is happening. It is happening for two reasons: First, as the scale of industrial agriculture increases, so does the scale of its abuses, and it is hard to hide large-scale abuses from consumers. It is virtually impossible now for intelligent consumers to be ignorant of the heartlessness and nastiness of animal confinement operations and their excessive use of antibiotics, of the use of hormones in meat and milk production, of the stenches and pollutants of pig and poultry factories, of the use of toxic chemicals and the waste of soil and soil health in industrial row-cropping, of the mysterious or disturbing or threatening practices associated with industrial food storage, preservation, and processing. Second, as the food industries focus more and more on gigantic global opportunities, they cannot help but overlook small local opportunities, as is made plain by the proliferation of "community-supported agriculture," farmers markets, health food stores, and so on. In fact, there are some markets that the great corporations by definition cannot supply. The market for so-called organic food, for example, is really a market for good, fresh, trustworthy food, food from producers known and trusted by consumers, and such food cannot be produced by a global corporation.

But the food economy is only one example. It is also possible to think of good local forest economies. And in the face of much neglect, it is possible to think of local small business economies—some of them related to the local economies of farm and forest—supported by locally owned, community-oriented banks.

What do these efforts of local economy have to do with conservation as we know it? The answer, I believe, is *everything*. The conservation movement, as I said earlier, has a conservation program; it has a preservation program; it has a rather sporadic health-protection program; but it has no economic program, and because it has no economic program it has the status of something exterior to daily life, surviving by emergency, like an ambulance service. In saying this, I do not mean to belittle the importance of protest, litigation, lobbying, legislation, large-scale organization—all of which I believe in and support. I am saying simply that we must do more. We must confront, on the ground, and each of us at home, the economic assumptions in which the problems of conservation originate.

We have got to remember that the great destructiveness of the industrial age comes from a division, a sort of divorce, in our economy, and therefore in our consciousness, between production and consumption. Of this radical division of functions we can say, without much fear of oversimplifying, that the aim of industrial producers is to sell as much as possible and that the aim of industrial consumers is to buy as much as possible. We need only to add that the aim of both producer and consumer is to be so far as possible care-free. Because of various pressures, governments have learned to coerce from producers some grudging concern for the health and solvency of consumers. No way has been found to coerce from consumers any consideration for the methods and sources of production.

What alerts consumers to the outrages of producers is typically some kind of loss or threat of loss. We see that in dividing consumption from production we have lost the function of conserving. Conserving is no longer an integral part of the economy of the producer or the consumer. Neither the producer nor the consumer any longer says, "I must be careful of this so that it will last." The working assumption of both is that where there is some, there must be more. If they can't get what they need in one place, they will find it in another. That is why conservation is now a separate concern and a separate effort.

But experience seems increasingly to be driving us out of the categories of producer and consumer and into the categories of citizen, family member, and community member, in all of which we have an inescapable interest in making things last. And here is where I think the conservation movement (I mean that movement that has defined itself as the defender of wilderness and the natural world) can involve itself in the fundamental issues of economy and land use, and in the process gain strength for its original causes.

I would like my fellow conservationists to notice how many people and organizations are now working to save something of value—not just wilderness places, wild rivers, wildlife habitat, species diversity, water quality, and air quality, but also agricultural land, family farms and ranches, communities, children and childhood, local schools, local economies, local food markets, livestock breeds and domestic plant varieties, fine old buildings, scenic roads, and so on. I would like my fellow conservationists to understand also that there is hardly a small farm or ranch or locally owned restaurant or store or shop or business anywhere that is not struggling to conserve itself.

All of these people, who are fighting sometimes lonely battles to keep things of value that they cannot bear to lose, are the conservation movement's natural allies. Most of them have the same enemies as the conservation movement. There is no necessary conflict among them. Thinking of them, in their great variety, in the essential likeness of their motives and concerns, one thinks of the possibility of a defined community of interest among them all, a shared stewardship of all the diversity of good things that are needed for the health and abundance of the world.

I don't suppose that this will be easy, given especially the history of conflict between conservationists and land users. I only suppose that it is necessary. Conservationists can't conserve everything that needs conserving without joining the effort to use well the agricultural lands, the forests, and the waters that we must use. To enlarge the areas protected from use without at the same time enlarging the areas of *good* use is a mistake. To have no large areas of protected old-growth forest would be folly, as most of us would agree. But it is also folly to have come this far in our history without a single working model of a thoroughly diversified and integrated, ecologically sound, local forest economy. That such an economy is possible is indicated by many imperfect or incomplete examples, but we need desperately to put the pieces together in one place—and then in every place.

The most tragic conflict in the history of conservation is that between the conservationists and the farmers and ranchers. It is tragic because it is unnecessary. There is no irresolvable conflict here, but the conflict that exists can be resolved only on the basis of a common understanding of good practice. Here again we need to foster and study working models: farms and ranches that are knowledgeably striving to bring economic practice into line with ecological reality, and local food economies in which consumers conscientiously support the best land stewardship.

We know better than to expect very soon a working model of a conserving global corporation. But we must begin to expect—and we must, as conservationists, begin working for, and in—working models of nature-conserving local economies. These are possible now. Good and able people are working hard to develop them now. They need the full support of the conservation movement now. Conservationists need to go to these people, ask what they can do to help, and then help. A little later, having helped, they can in turn ask for help.

(1996)

Stupidity in Concentration

I. Confinement, Concentration, Separation

M Y TASK HERE is to show the great stupidity of industrial animal production. Factory farms, like this essay, have the aim of cramming as much as possible into as small a space as possible. To understand these animal factories, we need to keep in mind three principles: confinement, concentration, and separation.

The principle of confinement in so-called animal science is derived from the industrial version of efficiency. The designers of animal factories appear to have had in mind the example of concentration camps or prisons, the aim of which is to house and feed the greatest number in the smallest space at the least expense of money, labor, and attention. To subject innocent creatures to such treatment has long been recognized as heartless. Animal factories make an economic virtue of heartlessness toward domestic animals, to which humans owe instead a large debt of respect and gratitude.

The defenders of animal factories typically assume, or wish others to assume, that these facilities concentrate animals only. But that is not so. They also concentrate the excrement of the animals—which, when properly dispersed, is a valuable source of fertility, but, when concentrated, is at best a waste, at worst a poison.

Perhaps even more dangerous is the inevitability that large concentrations of animals will invite concentrations of disease organisms, which in turn require concentrated and continuous use of antibiotics. And here the issue enlarges beyond the ecological problem to what some scientists think of as an evolutionary problem: The animal factory becomes a breeding ground for treatment-resistant pathogens, exactly as large field monocultures become breeding grounds for pesticide-resistant pests.

To concentrate food-producing animals in large numbers in one place inevitably separates them from the sources of their feed. Pasture and barnyard animals are removed from their old places in the order of a diversified farm, where they roamed about in some freedom, foraging to a significant extent for their own food, grazing in open pastures, or recycling barnyard and household wastes. Confined in the pens of animal factories, they are made dependent almost exclusively upon grains which are grown in large monocultures, at a now generally recognized ecological cost, and which must be transported to the animals sometimes over long distances. Animal factories are energy-wasting enterprises flourishing in a time when we need to be thinking of energy conservation.

The industrialization of agriculture, by concentration and separation, overthrows the restraints inherent in the diversity and balance of healthy ecosystems and good farms. This results in an unprecedented capacity for overproduction, which drives down farm income, which separates yet more farmers from their farms. For the independent farmers of the traditional small family farm, the animal factories substitute hired laborers, who at work are confined in the same unpleasant and unhealthy situation as the animals. Production at such a cost is temporary. The cost finally is diminishment of the human and ecological capacity to produce.

Animal factories ought to have been the subject of much government concern, *if* government is in fact concerned about the welfare of the land and the people. But, instead, the confined animal feeding industry has been the beneficiary of government encouragement and government incentives. This is the result of a political brain disease that causes people in power to think that anything that makes more money or "creates jobs" is good.

We have animal factories, in other words, because of a governmental addiction to short-term economics. Short-term economics is the practice of making as much money as you can as fast as you can by any possible means while ignoring the long-term effects. Short-term economics is the economics of self-interest and greed. People who operate on the basis of short-term economics accumulate large "externalized" costs, which they charge to the future—that is, to the world and to everybody's grandchildren.

People who are concerned about what their grandchildren will have to eat, drink, and breathe tend to be interested in long-term economics. Long-term economics involves a great deal besides the question of how to make a lot of money in a hurry. Long-term economists such as John Ikerd of the University of Missouri believe in applying "the Golden Rule across the generations—doing for future generations as we would have them do for us." Professor Ikerd says: "The three cornerstones of sustainability are ecological soundness, economic viability, and social justice." He thinks that animal factories are deficient by all three measures.

These factories raise issues of public health, of soil and water and air pollution, of the quality of human work, of the humane treatment of animals, of the proper ordering and conduct of agriculture, and the longevity and healthfulness of food production.

If the people in our state and national governments undertook to evaluate economic enterprises by the standards of long-term economics, they would have to employ their minds in actual thinking. For many of them, this would be a shattering experience, something altogether new, but it would also cause them to learn things and do things that would improve the lives of their constituents.

II. Factory Farms Versus Farms

Factory farms increase and concentrate the ecological risks of food production. This is a well-documented matter of fact. The rivers and estuaries of North Carolina, to use only one example, testify to how quickly a "private" animal factory can become an ecological catastrophe and a public liability.

A farm, on the other hand, disperses the ecological risks involved in food production. A *good* farm not only disperses these risks, but also minimizes them. On a good farm, ecological responsibility is inherent in proper methodologies of land management, and in correct balances between animals and acres, production and carrying capacity. A good farm does not put at risk the healthfulness of the land, the water, and the air.

The ecological differences between a factory farm and a farm may be paramount in a time of rapidly accelerating destruction of the natural world. But there is also an economic difference that, from the standpoint of human communities, is critical.

A factory farm locks the farmer in at the bottom of a corporate hierarchy. In return for the assumption of great economic and other risks, the farmer is permitted to participate minimally in the industry's earnings. In return, moreover, for the security of a contract with the corporation, the farmer gives up the farm's diversity and versatility, reducing it to a specialist operation with one use.

According to one company's projections, a farmer would buy into the broiler business at a cost of $624,275. That would be for four houses that would produce 506,000 birds per year. Under the company's terms, this investment would produce a yearly net income of $23,762. That would be an annual return on investment of 3.8 percent.

I don't know what percentage of annual return this company's shareholders expect to realize from *their* investment. I do know that if it is not substantially better than the farmer's percentage, they would be well advised to sell out and invest elsewhere.

The factory farm, rather than serving the farm family and the local community, is an economic siphon, sucking value out of the local landscape and the local community into distant bank accounts.

To entice them to buy Kentuckians' work and products so cheaply, our state government has given the animal confinement corporations some $200 million in state and federal tax "incentives." In gratitude for these gifts, these corporations now wish to be relieved of any mandated public liability or responsibility for their activities here.

I don't know that the arrogance and impudence of this has been equaled by any other industry. For not only have these people demonstrated, by their contempt for laws and regulations here and elsewhere, their intention to be bad neighbors; they come repeatedly before our elected representatives to ask for special exemptions. But in that very request they acknowledge the great risks and dangers that are involved in their way of doing business. Why should the innocent, why should people with a good conscience, want to be exempt from liability?

It is clear that the advocates of factory farming are not advocates of farming. They do not speak for farmers.

What they support is state-sponsored colonialism—government of, by, and for the corporations.

III. Sustainability

The word "sustainable" is well on its way to becoming a label, like the word "organic." And so I want to propose a definition of "sustainable agriculture." This phrase, I suggest, refers to a way of farming that can be continued indefinitely because it conforms to the terms imposed upon it by the nature of places and the nature of people.

Our present agriculture, in general, is not ecologically sustainable now, and it is a long way from becoming so. It is too toxic. It is too dependent on fossil fuels. It is too wasteful of soil, of soil fertility, and of water. It is destructive of the health of the natural systems that surround and support our economic life. And it is destructive of genetic diversity, both domestic and wild.

So far, these problems have not received enough attention from the news media or politicians, but the day is coming when they will. A great many people who know about agriculture are worrying about these problems already. It seems likely that the public, increasingly conscious of the issues of personal and ecological health, will sooner or later force the political leadership to pay attention. And a lot of farmers and grassroots farm organizations are now taking seriously the problem of ecological sustainability.

But there is a related issue that is even more neglected, one that has been largely obscured, even for people aware of the requirement of ecological sustainability, by the vogue of the so-called free market and the global economy. I am talking about the issue of the economic sustainability of farms and farmers, farm families and farm communities.

It ought to be obvious that in order to have sustainable agriculture, you have got to make sustainable the lives and livelihoods of the people who do the work. The land cannot thrive if the people who are its users and caretakers do not thrive. Ecological sustainability requires a complex *local* culture as the preserver of the necessary knowledge and skill; and this in turn requires a settled, stable, prosperous local population of farmers and other land users. It ought to be obvious that agriculture cannot be made sustainable by a dwindling population of economically depressed farmers and a growing population of migrant workers.

Why is our farm population dwindling away? Why are the still-surviving farms so frequently in desperate economic circumstances? Why is the suicide rate among farmers three times that of the country as a whole?

There is one reason that is paramount: The present agricultural economy, as designed by the agribusiness corporations (and the politicians, bureaucrats, economists, and experts who do their bidding), uses farmers as expendable "resources" in the process of production, the same way it uses the topsoil, the groundwater, and the ecological integrity of farm landscapes.

From the standpoint of sustainability, either of farmland or farm people, the present agricultural economy is a failure. It is, in fact, a catastrophe.

And there is no use in thinking that agriculture can become sustainable by better adapting to the terms imposed by this economy. That is hopeless, because its terms are the wrong terms. The purpose of this economy is rapid, short-term exploitation, not sustainability.

The story we are in now is exactly the same story we have been in for the last hundred years. It is the story of a fundamental conflict between the interests of farmers and farming and the interests of the agribusiness corporations. It is useless to suppose or pretend that this conflict does not exist, or to hope that you can somehow serve both sides at once. The interests are different, they are in conflict, and you have to get on one side or the other.

As a case in point, let us consider the economics of Kentucky's chicken factories, which some are pleased to look upon as a help to farmers. *The Courier-Journal* on May 28, 2000, told the story of a McLean County farmer who raises 1.2 million chickens a year. His borrowed investment of $750,000 brings him an annual income of $20,000 to $30,000. This declares itself immediately as a "deal" tailor-made for desperate farmers. Who besides a desperate farmer would see $20,000 or $30,000 as an acceptable annual return on an investment of $750,000 plus a year's work? In the poultry-processing corporations that sponsor such "farming," how many CEOs would see that as an acceptable return? The fact is that agriculture cannot be made sustainable in this way. The ecological risks are high, and the economic structure is forbidding. How many children of farmers in such an arrangement will want to farm?

Some people would like to claim that this sort of "economic development" is "inevitable." But the only things that seem inevitable about it are the corporate greed that motivates it and the careerism of the academic experts who try to justify it. On May 28, *The Courier-Journal* quoted an agribusiness apologist at the University of Kentucky's experiment station in Princeton, Gary Parker, who said in defense of the animal factories: "Agriculture is a high-volume, high-cost, high-risk type business. You have to borrow a tremendous amount of money. You have to generate a tremendous amount of income just to barely make a living."

The first problem with Mr. Parker's justification is that it amounts to a perfect condemnation of this kind of agriculture. In an editorial on June 4, *The Courier-Journal* quoted Mr. Parker, and then said that such agriculture, though compromising and risky, "can generate great rewards." *The Courier-Journal* did not say who would *get* those "great rewards." We may be sure, however, that they will not go to the farmers, who, according to Mr. Parker's confession, are just barely making a living.

The second problem with Mr. Parker's statement is that it is not necessarily true. In contrast to the factory farm that realizes a profit of $20,000 or $30,000 on the sale of 1,200,000 chickens, I know a farm family who last year, as a part of a diversified small farm enterprise, produced 2,000 pastured chickens for a net income of $6,000. This *farm* enterprise involved no large investment for housing or equipment, no large debt, no contract, and no environmental risk. The chickens were of excellent quality. The customers for them were ordinary citizens, about half of whom were from the local rural community. The demand far exceeds the supply. Most of the proceeds for these chickens went to the family that did the work of producing them. A substantial portion of that money will be spent in the local community. Such a possibility has not been noticed by Mr. Parker or *The Courier-Journal* because, I suppose, it is not "tremendous" and it serves the interest of farmers, not corporations.

(2002)

Watershed and Commonwealth

I LIVE AT THE LOWER END of the watershed of the Kentucky River, which drains a considerable portion of eastern and central Kentucky. After watching it daily and thinking about it for a long time, I cannot help but see my native river as a connector of places, regions, and people.

People who live at the lower ends of watersheds cannot be isolationists— or not for long. Pretty soon they will notice that water flows, and that will set them to thinking about the people upstream who either do or do not send down their silt and pollutants and garbage. Thinking about the people upstream ought to cause further thinking about the people downstream. Such pondering on the facts of gravity and the fluidity of water shows us that the golden rule speaks to a condition of absolute interdependency and obligation. People who live on rivers—or, in fact, anywhere in a watershed— might rephrase the rule in this way: Do unto those downstream as you would have those upstream do unto you. Rivers do not run upstream; we are not talking about economic reciprocity or a game of tit for tat. But it is not unthinkable that, depending on which way the wind blows, the downstream people may send the water back as acid rain.

Not long ago I scooped and hosed a good many pounds of displaced Kentucky soil out of my buildings. And though I have endeavored to keep my slopes well covered, I know that the same flood carried some of my own soil downstream. I mean to say that I speak here as one involved in a common wealth and a common fate, as one eligible to be involved in a common disaster, and as one of the guilty. The ethic (we could say the courtesy) of life in a watershed is unforgivingly practical; it has to be practiced or it does not exist. And like nearly everybody, I am not adequately skilled in that practice.

I have begun by speaking of the river both because it is itself a common wealth, and because it instructs us so unsparingly about the condition and the requirements of living in a common wealth. We have come to think of the word "commonwealth" as merely synonymous with "state" or "political body." I am attempting here to use the term in its literal sense, unfortunately obsolete, of the general welfare, the public good, the wealth that only can be held in common.

It is encouraging to see that, in thinking about their forests, Kentuckians are beginning to deal with the fact that the common wealth and private property are sometimes the same and sometimes are not. The original forests of the state, like its coal seams, were allowed to become private property without ever belonging to the common wealth. The same could be said of much of the state's agricultural economy. We know that Kentucky's economy began by producing goods to be sent down the rivers, and it has continued by sending the produce of the land (still usually "raw") out of the state by rail or road.

We can see, on the other hand, how a forest or farm or mine might belong both to a private owner and to the common wealth. This can happen if the enterprise is locally owned, if it is designed and understood as a part of the local economy, if it employs local people, if the local economy adds value to the product, if the enterprise upholds the highest standards of workmanship and stewardship, if it is properly scaled, and if its products serve local needs first.

Although it is easy to explain how conflicts between private interests and the common wealth came about in the past, I don't believe that it is easy to argue that such conflicts are unavoidable in the future. I believe that they can be avoided, but to avoid them we will have to begin now to think more carefully than we have done before.

To distinguish between private enterprises that exploit and diminish the common wealth and those that do not, we must answer fully and truly a few simple questions: What are the real, long-term costs of a particular enterprise—to investors, to people who are not investors, to the local community, and to nature? When the enterprise turns a profit, who gets the money? Where do the people live who get the money? How long does the money circulate within the local community before it leaves?

Even before they are answered, those are mind-changing questions. Once we have understood the importance of those questions, we will see that the most important dividing line in Kentucky is not geographic but demographic. This is the line between the people who are economically dependent on the local landscape and its products and the people who are not. Many of our people now share directly in the fate of the national or the global economy. They own shares in national or supranational corporations, or they work for corporations or governments whose activities, wherever they are, are not primarily local. On the other side of the line, we have people whose economic fate is indissolubly bound to and limited by the fate of the local landscape.

We know that during the century now ending enormous wealth has been produced from the land of Kentucky and by the work of the people of Kentucky. And we know that the production of this wealth has impoverished the land, the rural communities, and the working people. At this point, a lot of people will want to draw a regional line: "Yes, but it has been worse in eastern Kentucky." And I will agree, but only with a qualification: It has been worse in eastern Kentucky, but only because the process of industrial degradation has been *faster* in eastern Kentucky. You can ruin land and communities faster with an industrial economy of coal than you can with an industrial economy of agriculture. Aside from the issue of speed, industrial mining and industrial agriculture are in principle the same. Their common purpose is to extract the most wealth in the least time at the lowest cost, and to discount altogether the ecological and social costs. If, anywhere in Kentucky, you see sloping land being row-cropped year after year, you are looking at land being ruined. Its ruination is not so eye-catching and dramatic as that of a strip mine, but the result will be the same—exhaustion and sterility—and it is happening plenty fast. If, anywhere in Kentucky, you see a small town with its commercial buildings empty, its school closed, and its last homegrown doctor retired or dead, you are looking at community disintegration as the direct result of an extractive economy, and what region it is in does not matter.

We are well-acquainted with the effects on the land and people of eastern Kentucky of the absentee ownership of the coal industry and of that industry's boom-and-bust cycles. But what about other rural areas of the state? In those areas soil is washing away, small towns are dying, the farm population is rapidly declining, and farm-related businesses are failing. For the reason why, we need look no further than the following facts about the state's most favored and fortunate crop: "In 1980, U.S. growers received 7 cents of the consumer tobacco dollar. In 1991, they received less than 3 cents. In contrast, manufacturers and wholesalers-retailers received 59 cents in

1980, and 73 cents in 1991" (Verner N. Grise, "The Changing Tobacco User's Dollar," *Tobacco Situation and Outlook*, Sept. 1995, p. 35). I should add that, beyond the farm towns of the tobacco-producing states, the tobacco industry is neither local nor even primarily dependent on tobacco. The point is obvious: In a national and increasingly international industrial economy, the land-dependent people who do the actual work of production are served last; their places and communities are served not at all. The working people of the eastern Kentucky coalfields get the smallest share of the income that depends on their work and their land, and this is true of the working people of the other rural areas of our state. They all suck the hind tit.

The catch is that this is bad for everybody. Even the richest beneficiaries of the present economy cannot prosper indefinitely in a country, or a world, of devastated landscapes populated by the poor, the exploited, and the unemployed. Finally, the bills will be delivered, and everybody will pay.

When your community loses a school, a church, a doctor, a grocery or hardware store, a restaurant, or a garage, what does that cost you and your community, starting with mileage? When a Wal-Mart comes in and captures the trade of several stores in several towns, what does that cost in travel, convenience, neighborliness, community integrity, economic diversity? Some of this cannot be computed. But some can, and nobody is computing it. However, it is getting easier for country people simply to *see* that the farther away from home you go to spend your money, the less you have to come home to.

I said earlier that if, in the future, we are to avoid ruinous conflicts between private interests and the common wealth, then we must think more carefully now. It certainly is possible to think better than we have in the past, but it will not be easy. The difficulty will be in finding our way past certain ideas that are supposed to be helping us to think but in fact are paralyzing our minds. I am thinking of such ideas as "technological progress," "the global economy," "job creation," and "bringing in industry." These ideas all are related. The problem with them is that our leaders speak of them as if they are solutions, when in fact they are problems.

Technological progress is advertised to us as a sequence of solutions. The problem with technological progress may be stated as a question: How much of the gain is net? The sellers of technology want us to believe that the net is one hundred percent. If we are awake, we know that there is always a cost. If we study examples, we know that sometimes the solution proves a bigger problem than the problem we started with. We know too that technologists sometimes provide solutions to problems that do not exist.

We assume that technology somehow determines the quality of work, which ultimately is to say the quality of land use. But that is not so—at least, on a relatively modest scale it is not so. We know that land can be ruined or improved by simple technology. What technology does determine, in this industrial age, is who gets the money. If the local people who do the work do not get the money, or at least a fair share of it, then the work will be done poorly and the land will be ill-used. It is only after the local standards of work and of life have been debased or overpowered by an absentee or colonial economy that large-scale technology can be introduced, and large-scale technology does determine the quality of work in the sense that it limits how well it can be done. This is why "handmade" has become a term of praise.

What we call technological progress has made possible the "global economy," which exists solely to meet the demands and fill the bank accounts of capital-intensive, highly mobile international corporations. It is a system by which these corporations procure raw materials and labor wherever they are cheapest and sell their finished products wherever the consumers are richest and most gullible. Thus Nike can pay starvation wages to teenage girls in Vietnam to make sneakers that will be sold at outrageous prices to the affluent and fashion-crazed teenagers of the United States.

At present, the unquestioned assumption of our political leaders is that our exclusive economic and educational goal must be to "compete in the global economy." What does this mean? It means that we have to undersell the competition everywhere in the world. Is this what we want? Do we really want our national and state governments to function as marketing agencies to sell our natural resources and our working people at the lowest price?

"But this will create jobs," our leaders say, forgetting to say (if they have ever asked) what kinds of jobs; and forgetting (if they have ever known) that they are depending for "job creation" on an industrial enterprise whose chief goal for two hundred years has been job elimination. If you want an idea of the real status of "job creation" in our economy, just notice how much time you are spending on the telephone in listening to a machine tell you things you don't want to know. The first rule of industrialism is to get work done as cheaply as possible, whether or not this entails the impoverishment of workers or the elimination of jobs.

Nevertheless, in order to "create jobs" our political leaders are obsessed with the idea of "bringing in industry." I have been told that every state has a program for "bringing in industry." It is now imaginable that every nation, province, and municipality on earth is panting to "bring in industry." But this raises some interesting questions: Why? Where from? And at what cost? Is there any alternative to bidding for the favors of large out-of-state corporations with "incentives"? *Must* we pay bureaucrats to give our money away and undersell our labor and resources so that we can have jobs?

Well, maybe so. I don't want to give the impression that I know all the answers, or even that I would like to know them all. But I am interested in preserving the common wealth—the land and the people—of Kentucky. I don't see how this can be done if we Kentuckians don't develop strong, stable, land-and-people-conserving local economies, making the most of local investment, local labor, local loyalty, local diversity, and local caretaking. I think that real jobs—which is to say vocations, callings, lives of work, and working lives—are offered and preserved only by such economies.

I am not suggesting that we ought to be isolated, economically or culturally. I understand the need for imports and exports, comings and goings, exchanges and minglings of all kinds. On the other hand, I don't want the abilities, the legitimate hopes, and the responsibilities of our people, or the productive capacity of our land, to be overlooked or undervalued in our haste to keep up with the fashions of thought.

Gurney Norman recently gave me a copy of a most interesting book, *Carcassone*, by Clifton Caudill of Carcassone in Letcher County. I liked very much Mr. Caudill's account of the way his father went about starting the school at Carcassone in 1920. Money was scarce, but there was no thought of government help or expert advice. Mr. Caudill's father contracted to build a mile of road for $5,000. With the profit from the road job, he bought a sawmill to saw lumber from trees cut on his own farm, and with the lumber he and his neighbors built the school. Is this community spirit of self-help and free enterprise now dead among our people? Maybe it is. Maybe all we can do now is just sit and wait for help—but I hate to think so. I would like us to see what we can do for ourselves.

Before running off in all directions to embrace the global economy and bring in industry, I would want to ask and try to answer several questions:

What do we need in Kentucky that we are not producing here but that we *could* produce here? What do we produce here that we could use here but are shipping elsewhere? What are Kentuckians now paying in transportation and other costs for such needless exporting and importing? Is there any way for a locality or even a state to control, in the interest of its own people, an economy based on the export of raw products from the countryside? Is there any way to assure that a brought-in industry will make common cause with the local community and act in the best interest of the local landscape? Has any brought-in industry ever done this? If so, where is the accounting? Is there any law that says that all industrial enterprises must be big and brought-in? How might we employ the industry and the intelligence and the talents of our working people and at the same time assure to them an equitable share in the common wealth? How might we finance with local capital the development of small-scale, nonpolluting local industries to add value to the products of our farms and forests? Are there, anywhere, working examples of such enterprises? If so, could we have a look at their accounting?

As a taxpayer, I would gladly pay my share and more for full and fair answers to such questions. I think that an effort to find the answers would serve well all the people and all the land of our Commonwealth—east, west, and middle, upstream and down.

(1997)

The Agrarian Standard

THE UNSETTLING OF AMERICA was published twenty-five years ago; it is still in print and is still being read. As its author, I am tempted to be glad of this, and yet, if I believe what I said in that book, and I still do, then I should be anything but glad. The book would have had a far happier fate if it could have been disproved or made obsolete years ago.

It remains true because the conditions it describes and opposes, the abuses of farmland and farming people, have persisted and become worse over the last twenty-five years. In 2002 we have less than half the number of farmers in the United States that we had in 1977. Our farm communities are far worse off now than they were then. Our soil erosion rates continue to be unsustainably high. We continue to pollute our soils and streams with agricultural poisons. We continue to lose farmland to urban development of the most wasteful sort. The large agribusiness corporations that were mainly national in 1977 are now global, and are replacing the world's agricultural diversity, useful primarily to farmers and local consumers, with bioengineered and patented monocultures that are merely profitable to corporations. The purpose of this new global economy, as Vandana Shiva has rightly said, is to replace "food democracy" with a worldwide "food dictatorship."

To be an agrarian writer in such a time is an odd experience. One keeps writing essays and speeches that one would prefer not to write, that one wishes would prove unnecessary, that one hopes nobody will have any need for in twenty-five years. My life as an agrarian writer has certainly involved me in such confusions, but I have never doubted for a minute the importance of the hope I have tried to serve: the hope that we might become a healthy people in a healthy land.

We agrarians are involved in a hard, long, momentous contest, in which we are so far, and by a considerable margin, the losers. What we have undertaken to defend is the complex accomplishment of knowledge, cultural memory, skill, self-mastery, good sense, and fundamental decency—the high and indispensable art—for which we probably can find no better name than "good farming." I mean farming as defined by agrarianism as opposed to farming as defined by industrialism: farming as the proper use and care of an immeasurable gift.

I believe that this contest between industrialism and agrarianism now defines the most fundamental human difference, for it divides not just two nearly opposite concepts of agriculture and land use, but also two nearly opposite ways of understanding ourselves, our fellow creatures, and our world.

The way of industrialism is the way of the machine. To the industrial mind, a machine is not merely an instrument for doing work or amusing ourselves or making war; it is an explanation of the world and of life. The machine's entirely comprehensible articulation of parts defines the acceptable meanings of our experience, and it prescribes the kinds of meanings the industrial scientists and scholars expect to discover. These meanings have to do with nomenclature, classification, and rather short lineages of causation. Because industrialism cannot understand living things except as machines, and can grant them no value that is not utilitarian, it conceives of farming and forestry as forms of mining; it cannot use the land without abusing it.

Industrialism prescribes an economy that is placeless and displacing. It does not distinguish one place from another. It applies its methods and technologies indiscriminately in the American East and the American West, in the United States and in India. It thus continues the economy of colonialism. The shift of colonial power from European monarchy to global corporation is perhaps the dominant theme of modern history. All along— from the European colonization of Africa, Asia, and the New World, to the domestic colonialism of American industries, to the colonization of the entire rural world by the global corporations—it has been the same story of the gathering of an exploitive economic power into the hands of a few people who are alien to the places and the people they exploit. Such an economy is bound to destroy locally adapted agrarian economies everywhere it goes, simply because it is too ignorant not to do so. And it has succeeded precisely to the extent that it has been able to inculcate the same ignorance in workers and consumers. A part of the function of industrial education is to preserve and protect this ignorance.

To the corporate and political and academic servants of global industrialism, the small family farm and the small farming community are not known, are not imaginable, and are therefore unthinkable, except as damaging stereotypes. The people of "the cutting edge" in science, business, education, and politics have no patience with the local love, local loyalty, and local knowledge that make people truly native to their places and therefore good caretakers of their places. This is why one of the primary principles in industrialism has always been to get the worker away from home. From the beginning it has been destructive of home employment and home economies. The office or the factory or the institution is the place for work. The economic function of the household has been increasingly the consumption of purchased goods. Under industrialism, the farm too has become increasingly consumptive, and farms fail as the costs of consumption overpower the income from production.

The idea of people working at home, as family members, as neighbors, as natives and citizens of their places, is as repugnant to the industrial mind as the idea of self-employment. The industrial mind is an organizational mind, and I think this mind is deeply disturbed and threatened by the existence of people who have no boss. This may be why people with such minds, as they approach the top of the political hierarchy, so readily sell themselves to "special interests." They cannot bear to be unbossed. They cannot stand the lonely work of making up their own minds.

The industrial contempt for anything small, rural, or natural translates into contempt for uncentralized economic systems, any sort of local self-sufficiency in food or other necessities. The industrial "solution" for such systems is to increase the scale of work and trade. It is to bring Big Ideas, Big Money, and Big Technology into small rural communities, economies, and ecosystems—the brought-in industry and the experts being invariably alien to and contemptuous of the places to which they are brought in. There is never any question of propriety, of adapting the thought or the purpose or the technology to the place.

The result is that problems correctable on a small scale are replaced by large-scale problems for which there are no large-scale corrections. Meanwhile, the large-scale enterprise has reduced or destroyed the possibility of small-scale corrections. This exactly describes our present agriculture.

Forcing all agricultural localities to conform to economic conditions imposed from afar by a few large corporations has caused problems of the largest possible scale, such as soil loss, genetic impoverishment, and groundwater pollution, which are correctable only by an agriculture of locally adapted, solar-powered, diversified small farms—a correction that, after a half century of industrial agriculture, will be difficult to achieve.

The industrial economy thus is inherently violent. It impoverishes one place in order to be extravagant in another, true to its colonialist ambition. A part of the "externalized" cost of this is war after war.

Industrialism begins with technological invention. But agrarianism begins with givens: land, plants, animals, weather, hunger, and the birthright knowledge of agriculture. Industrialists are always ready to ignore, sell, or destroy the past in order to gain the entirely unprecedented wealth, comfort, and happiness supposedly to be found in the future. Agrarian farmers know that their very identity depends on their willingness to receive gratefully, use responsibly, and hand down intact an inheritance, both natural and cultural, from the past. Agrarians understand themselves as the users and caretakers of some things they did not make, and of some things that they cannot make.

I said a while ago that to agrarianism farming is the proper use and care of an immeasurable gift. The shortest way to understand this, I suppose, is the religious way. Among the commonplaces of the Bible, for example, are the admonitions that the world was made and approved by God, that it belongs to Him, and that its good things come to us from Him as gifts. Beyond those ideas is the idea that the whole Creation exists only by participating in the life of God, sharing in His being, breathing His breath. "The world," Gerard Manley Hopkins said, "is charged with the grandeur of God." Such thoughts seem strange to us now, and what has estranged us from them is our economy. The industrial economy could not have been derived from such thoughts any more than it could have been derived from the golden rule.

If we believed that the existence of the world is rooted in mystery and in sanctity, then we would have a different economy. It would still be an economy of use, necessarily, but it would be an economy also of return. The economy would have to accommodate the need to be worthy of the gifts we receive and use, and this would involve a return of propitiation, praise, gratitude, responsibility, good use, good care, and a proper regard for future generations. What is most conspicuously absent from the industrial economy and industrial culture is this idea of return. Industrial humans relate themselves to the world and its creatures by fairly direct acts of violence. Mostly we take without asking, use without respect or gratitude, and give nothing in return. Our economy's most voluminous product is waste—valuable materials irrecoverably misplaced, or randomly discharged as poisons.

To perceive the world and our life in it as gifts originating in sanctity is to see our human economy as a continuing moral crisis. Our life of need and work forces us inescapably to use in time things belonging to eternity, and to assign finite values to things already recognized as infinitely valuable. This is a fearful predicament. It calls for prudence, humility, good work, propriety of scale. It calls for the complex responsibilities of caretaking and giving-back that we mean by "stewardship." To all of this the idea of the immeasurable value of the resource is central.

We can get to the same idea by a way a little more economic and practical, and this is by following through our literature the ancient theme of the small farmer or husbandman who leads an abundant life on a scrap of land often described as cast-off or poor. This figure makes his first literary appearance, so far as I know, in Virgil's Fourth Georgic:

> I saw a man,
> An old Cilician, who occupied
> An acre or two of land that no one wanted,
> A patch not worth the ploughing, unrewarding
> For flocks, unfit for vineyards; he however
> By planting here and there among the scrub
> Cabbages or white lilies and verbena
> And flimsy poppies, fancied himself a king
> In wealth, and coming home late in the evening
> Loaded his board with unbought delicacies.

Virgil's old squatter, I am sure, is a literary outcropping of an agrarian theme that has been carried from earliest times until now mostly in family or folk tradition, not in writing, though other such people can be found in books. Wherever found, they don't vary by much from Virgil's prototype. They don't have or require a lot of land, and the land they have is often marginal. They practice subsistence agriculture, which has been much derided by agricultural economists and other learned people of the industrial age, and they always associate frugality with abundance.

In my various travels, I have seen a number of small homesteads like that of Virgil's old farmer, situated on "land that no one wanted" and yet abundantly productive of food, pleasure, and other goods. And especially in my younger days, I was used to hearing farmers of a certain kind say, "They may run me out, but they won't starve me out" or "I may get shot, but I'm not going to starve." Even now, if they cared, I think agricultural economists could find small farmers who have prospered, not by "getting big," but by practicing the ancient rules of thrift and subsistence, by accepting the limits of their small farms, and by knowing well the value of having a little land.

How do we come at the value of a little land? We do so, following this strand of agrarian thought, by reference to the value of *no* land. Agrarians value land because somewhere back in the history of their consciousness is the memory of being landless. This memory is implicit, in Virgil's poem, in the old farmer's happy acceptance of "an acre or two of land that no one wanted." If you have no land you have nothing: no food, no shelter, no warmth, no freedom, no life. If we remember this, we know that all economies begin to lie as soon as they assign a fixed value to land. People who have been landless know that the land is invaluable; it is worth everything. Preagricultural humans, of course, knew this too. And so, evidently, do the animals. It is a fearful thing to be without a "territory." Whatever the market may say, the worth of the land is what it always was: It is worth what food, clothing, shelter, and freedom are worth; it is worth what life is worth. This perception moved the settlers from the Old World into the New. Most of our American ancestors came here because they knew what it was to be landless; to be landless was to be threatened by want and also by enslavement. Coming here, they bore the ancestral memory of serfdom. Under feudalism, the few who owned the land owned also, by an inescapable political logic, the people who worked the land.

Thomas Jefferson, who knew all these things, obviously was thinking of them when he wrote in 1785 that "it is not too soon to provide by every possible means that as few as possible shall be without a little portion of land. The small landholders are the most precious part of a state. . . ." He was saying, two years before the adoption of our Constitution, that a democratic state and democratic liberties depend upon democratic ownership of the land. He was already anticipating and fearing the division of our people into settlers, the people who wanted "a little portion of land" as a home, and, virtually opposite to those, the consolidators and exploiters of the land and the land's wealth, who would not be restrained by what Jefferson called "the natural affection of the human mind." He wrote as he did in 1785 because he feared exactly the political theory that we now have: the idea that government exists to guarantee the right of the most wealthy to own or control the land without limit.

In any consideration of agrarianism, this issue of limitation is critical. Agrarian farmers see, accept, and live within their limits. They understand and agree to the proposition that there is "this much and no more." Everything that happens on an agrarian farm is determined or conditioned by the understanding that there is only so much land, so much water in the cistern, so much hay in the barn, so much corn in the crib, so much firewood in the shed, so much food in the cellar or freezer, so much strength in the back and arms—and no more. This is the understanding that induces thrift, family coherence, neighborliness, local economies. Within accepted limits, these virtues become necessities. The agrarian sense of abundance comes from the experienced possibility of frugality and renewal within limits.

This is exactly opposite to the industrial idea that abundance comes from the violation of limits by personal mobility, extractive machinery, long-distance transport, and scientific or technological breakthroughs. If we use up the good possibilities in this place, we will import goods from some other place, or we will go to some other place. If nature releases her wealth too slowly, we will take it by force. If we make the world too toxic for honeybees, some compound brain, Monsanto perhaps, will invent tiny robots that will fly about, pollinating flowers and making honey.

To be landless in an industrial society obviously is not at all times to be jobless and homeless. But the ability of the industrial economy to provide jobs and homes depends on prosperity, and on a very shaky kind of prosperity too. It depends on "growth" of the wrong things such as roads and dumps and poisons—on what Edward Abbey called "the ideology of the cancer cell"—and on greed with purchasing power. In the absence of growth, greed, and affluence, the dependents of an industrial economy too easily suffer the consequences of having no land: joblessness, homelessness, and want. This is not a theory. We have seen it happen.

I don't think that being landed necessarily means owning land. It does mean being connected to a home landscape from which one may live by the interactions of a local economy and without the routine intervention of governments, corporations, or charities.

In our time it is useless and probably wrong to suppose that a great many urban people ought to go out into the countryside and become home-steaders or farmers. But it is not useless or wrong to suppose that urban people have agricultural responsibilities that they should try to meet. And in fact this is happening. The agrarian population among us is growing, and by no means is it made up merely of some farmers and some country people. It includes urban gardeners, urban consumers who are buying food from local farmers, organizers of local food economies, consumers who have grown doubtful of the healthfulness, the trustworthiness, and the dependability of the corporate food system—people, in other words, who understand what it means to be landless.

Apologists for industrial agriculture rely on two arguments. In one of them, they say that the industrialization of agriculture, and its dominance by corporations, has been "inevitable." It has come about and it continues by the agency of economic and technological determinism. There has been simply nothing that anybody could do about it.

The other argument is that industrial agriculture has come about by choice, inspired by compassion and generosity. Seeing the shadow of mass starvation looming over the world, the food conglomerates, the machinery companies, the chemical companies, the seed companies, and the other suppliers of "purchased inputs" have done all that they have done in order to solve "the problem of hunger" and to "feed the world."

We need to notice, first, that these two arguments, often used and perhaps believed by the same people, exactly contradict each other. Second, though supposedly it has been imposed upon the world by economic and technological forces beyond human control, industrial agriculture has been pretty consistently devastating to nature, to farmers, and to rural communities, at the same time that it has been highly profitable to the agribusiness corporations, which have submitted not quite reluctantly to its "inevitability." And, third, tearful over human suffering as they always have been, the agribusiness corporations have maintained a religious faith in the profitability of their charity. They have instructed the world that it is better for people to buy food from the corporate global economy than to raise it for themselves. What is the proper solution to hunger? Not food from the local landscape, but industrial development. After decades of such innovative thought, hunger is still a worldwide calamity.

The primary question for the corporations, and so necessarily for us, is not how the world will be fed, but who will control the land, and therefore the wealth, of the world. If the world's people accept the industrial premises that favor bigness, centralization, and (for a few people) high profitability, then the corporations will control all of the world's land and all of its wealth. If, on the contrary, the world's people might again see the advantages of local economies, in which people live, so far as they are able to do so, from their home landscapes, and work patiently toward that end, eliminating waste and the cruelties of landlessness and homelessness, then I think they might reasonably hope to solve "the problem of hunger," and several other problems as well.

But do the people of the world, allured by TV, supermarkets, and big cars, or by dreams thereof, *want* to live from their home landscapes? *Could they do so,* if they wanted to? Those are hard questions, not readily answerable by anybody. Throughout the industrial decades, people have become increasingly and more numerously ignorant of the issues of land use, of food, clothing, and shelter. What would they do, and what *could* they do, if they were forced by war or some other calamity to live from their home landscapes?

It is a fact, well attested but little noticed, that our extensive, mobile, highly centralized system of industrial agriculture is extremely vulnerable to acts of terrorism. It will be hard to protect an agriculture of genetically impoverished monocultures that is entirely dependent on cheap petroleum and long-distance transportation. We know too that the great corporations, which grow and act so far beyond the restraint of "the natural affections of the human mind," are vulnerable to the natural depravities of the human mind, such as greed, arrogance, and fraud.

The agricultural industrialists like to say that their agrarian opponents are merely sentimental defenders of ways of farming that are hopelessly old-fashioned, justly dying out. Or they say that their opponents are the victims, as Richard Lewontin put it, of "a false nostalgia for a way of life that never existed." But these are not criticisms. They are insults.

For agrarians, the correct response is to stand confidently on our fundamental premise, which is both democratic and ecological: The land is a gift of immeasurable value. If it is a gift, then it is a gift to all the living in all time. To withhold it from some is finally to destroy it for all. For a few powerful people to own or control it all, or decide its fate, is wrong.

From that premise we go directly to the question that begins the agrarian agenda and is the discipline of all agrarian practice: What is the best way to use land? Agrarians know that this question necessarily has many answers, not just one. We are not asking what is the best way to farm everywhere in the world, or everywhere in the United States, or everywhere in Kentucky or Iowa. We are asking what is the best way to farm in each one of the world's numberless places, as defined by topography, soil type, climate, ecology, history, culture, and local need. And we know that the standard cannot be determined only by market demand or productivity or profitability or technological capability, or by any other single measure, however important it may be. The agrarian standard, inescapably, is local adaptation, which requires bringing local nature, local people, local economy, and local culture into a practical and enduring harmony.

(2002)

Still Standing

I N 1930, a group of young men calling themselves "Twelve Southerners"
published a book unique in American literature. Entitled *I'll Take My
Stand,* the book contained an essay by each of the twelve: John Crowe Ransom, Donald Davidson, Frank Lawrence Owsley, John Gould Fletcher, Lyle
H. Lanier, Allen Tate, Herman Clarence Nixon, Andrew Nelson Lytle,
Robert Penn Warren, John Donald Wade, Henry Blue Kline, and Stark
Young. This group, known as the Southern (or the Nashville or the Vanderbilt) Agrarians, grew out of the mutuality of a gathering of poets, the
"Fugitives," who conversed and wrote in Nashville in the 1920's. Four of the
Fugitives—Ransom, Davidson, Tate, and Warren—contributed essays to
I'll Take My Stand.

John Crowe Ransom, in addition to his own essay, contributed an introduction, "A Statement of Principles," to which all of the twelve subscribed.
Among the agreed-upon principles are the following:

"The capitalization of the applied sciences has now become extravagant
and uncritical. . . ."

"The contribution that science can make to a labor is to render it easier
by the help of a tool or a process, and to assure the laborer of his perfect
economic security while he is engaged upon it. . . . But the modern
laborer has not exactly received this benefit under the industrial regime.
His labor is hard, its tempo is fierce, and his employment is insecure."

"The regular act of applied science is to introduce into labor a labor-saving device or a machine. Whether this is a benefit depends on how far
advisable it is to save the labor. . . . The act of labor as one of the happy
functions of human life has been in effect abandoned. . . ."

"... some economic evils follow in the wake of the machines. These are such as overproduction, unemployment, and a growing inequality in the distribution of wealth. But the remedies proposed by the apologists are always homeopathic. They expect the evils to disappear when we have bigger and better machines, and more of them."

"We have more time in which to consume, and many more products to be consumed. But the tempo of our labors communicates itself to our satisfactions, and these also become brutal and hurried."

"The modern man has lost his sense of vocation."

"We receive the illusion of having power over nature. . . . The God of nature under these conditions is merely an amiable expression, a super-fluity. . . ."

"Art depends, in general, like religion, on a right attitude to nature. . . ."

"We cannot recover our native humanism by adopting some standard of taste that is critical enough to question the contemporary arts but not critical enough to question the social and economic life which is their ground."

"... a fresh labor-saving device introduced into an industry does not emancipate the laborers in that industry so much as it evicts them. Applied at the expense of agriculture, for example, the new processes have reduced the part of the population supporting itself upon the soil to a smaller and smaller fraction."

"Opposed to the industrial society is the agrarian. . . . The theory of agrarianism is that the culture of the soil is the best and most sensitive of vocations, and that therefore it should have the economic preference and enlist the maximum number of workers."

The twelve essays that follow "A Statement of Principles" vary considerably in quality, in readability, and in what might be called their arguability. That surviving agrarians (and others too) may find them interesting, instructive, useful, and in some ways indispensable does not set them beyond the need for exacting criticism.

I wouldn't put "A Statement of Principles" beyond criticism, either. I have read it many times, inevitably bringing to it the privilege of hindsight, and in the light of that later knowledge, wishing to alter or clarify some of its sentences. It is nonetheless the supreme declaration of the book, as it ought to be. It has held up startlingly well. If I were to attempt to revise it, I would do so only with the consciousness that its main points are more obviously true now than they were in 1930. As it stands, I know of no criticism of industrial assumptions that can equal it in clarity, economy, and eloquence.

That "A Statement of Principles" has never been widely read and discussed is a great misfortune for our country. But then, *I'll Take My Stand* is a misfortunate book. It is a book that called for a sequel; it was meant to have an influence and a practical result. Its tragedy, and ours, is that its challenge was never taken up. By the fall of 1931, as J. A. Bryant Jr. writes in *Twentieth Century Southern Literature*, its twelve authors "were compelled to acknowledge that *I'll Take My Stand* had been at best a shaky beginning for what the more ardent among them had hoped might be a crusade." They had hoped, as they said, to become "members of a national agrarian movement." That movement did not take place. What took place, instead, was the all-out industrialization of American agriculture, south and north.

The reputation and influence of the book have been reduced also because it was written during the era of segregation. None of the authors at that time had explicitly dissociated himself from racism, and at least one of them never did so. Donald Davidson was to the last a segregationist, and this brings us, as readers, to trial, just as it does Davidson. We must decide whether to deal with this issue according to the rules of political correctness or according to the rules of critical discourse. The enterprise of political correctness deals in the political merchandise of general categories, invoking judgment without trial, whereas critical discourse must try to deal intelligently with the fact that people who are wrong about one thing may be right about another. And in fact Donald Davidson the segregationist contributed to *I'll Take My Stand* an excellent essay on the meaning of the arts in an industrial society.

A further misfortune of that book was the migration of the most prominent of its authors to universities outside their region. Some of them proceeded to renounce or abandon their old allegiance to agrarian principles, and one who did so was the author of the "Statement of Principles," John Crowe Ransom. Writing in the *Kenyon Review*, in 1945, Ransom dismissed the 1930 collaboration as "the agrarian nostalgia." He went on to say that "without consenting to division of labor, and hence modern society, we should have not only no effective science, invention, and scholarship, but nothing to speak of in art, e.g., Reviews and contributions to Reviews, fine poems and their exegesis.... The pure though always divided knowledges, and the physical gadgets and commodities, constitute our science, and are the guilty fruits; but the former are triumphs of muscular intellect, and the latter at best are clean and wholly at our service."

To me, it is impossible to compare the above passage with the sentences from the "Statement of Principles" quoted earlier and not feel that John Crowe Ransom's elegant mind had somehow taken leave of the practical world. These, the key sentences of his recantation, would seem merely credulous and silly, except that they affirm the dependence of modern academic life upon the economy of industrialism, a dependence that has continued and grown worse.

And so we come, by a progression all too logical, to the greatest and most troubling misfortune of *I'll Take My Stand:* namely, that of the twelve authors, seven—Ransom, Davidson, Fletcher, Tate, Lytle, Warren, and Young—were or came to be well known as writers or poets or men of letters. Given only rationality and the ordinary meanings of words, a person would suppose that this literary prominence would have caused the agrarian principles of their book to be taken seriously by intelligent readers. But so straightforward an assumption overlooks the easy compatibility, acknowledged by Ransom, between the industrial economy and the modern university.

Nobody, of course, would have expected *I'll Take My Stand* to be taken seriously in the colleges of agriculture, where "agri-industry" was largely invented and where it has been for two generations a fanatically conventional "science." But the English departments, too, seem to have felt that something needed to be done to fend off the agrarianism of the Agrarians. Ransom's 1945 essay had simply told the truth. What would we do for "Reviews and contributions to Reviews, fine poems and their exegesis" (not to mention professorships, endowed chairs, sabbatical leaves, conferences, grants, and fellowships—all the "necessities" of the modern academic life) if it were not for the taxes and the charity of the industrialists? And so there followed a merely predictable anxiety to avoid acknowledging the least hint of practical or practicable truth in the Agrarians' attack upon industrialism and their defense of agrarianism.

The English departments were unable to ignore the literary members of the twelve as writers. They were finally too prominent—and too readily available to the literary industries of poetry and exegesis—for dismissal. The problem was rather too neatly resolved by the New Criticism (formulated in part by Ransom and Warren), which proposed that the reader's attention should be focused upon "the text" of a work of literature to the exclusion of everything outside the text. This was, within limits, useful; all of us who came of age under the influence of the New Criticism are, within limits, indebted to it. But the New Criticism also afforded a way to take a writer's work seriously "as literature," questioning minutely *how* it says what it says, while ignoring or dismissing the question of whether or not what it says is true.

I'll Take My Stand thus began to be read as a literary "text." The authors, these readers held, did not mean to be saying anything political or practical or economic. They did not mean to be taken seriously even by other agrarians. They really did not know what they were doing when they called themselves agrarians. Their agrarianism was merely symbolic or metaphorical, a kind of poetry, only literature. (Martin Luther King, Jr.'s "Letter from Birmingham Jail," so far as I know, has not yet been read in this way—though it *can* be; the Sermon on the Mount is read, by some, "as literature.") This making into literature, and literature alone, of a serious argument on a serious—and *still* serious—issue rests necessarily upon the assumption, which is well nigh universal among the academic intellectuals who are aware of the subject at all, that industrial agriculture has made every nonindustrial kind of agriculture obsolete.

I don't think anybody in particular can be blamed for this. The fault lies with the sort of organizational norms and conventions that have the power to exclude knowledge and ideas even from institutions of higher learning. This exclusiveness may not be apparent from the point of view of the universities. It is certainly apparent, however, from the point of view of anybody whose eye is at all close to the ground—a person, let us say, in a country community who is thinking about the requirements for good farming, good soil stewardship, and the survival of our remnant farm population. Such a person will see without much trouble that in all the talk about agrarians

and agrarianism, agri-industry and agri-business, what has been left out of
account is the future of the land, of farmers, and thus of eating. Nonindustrial, land- and people-conserving ways of agriculture have simply been
ignored, even though a great many such ways are still being successfully
practiced in the United States and elsewhere right now.

But this willingness of literary critics to read a serious and competent
argument as a "text" or "only literature" is not merely a way of ignoring
issues; it is also a way of depriving literature of its moral or cultural or religious force. Writers can write only uselessly against evils if what they write
is read "as literature," which by the critics' definition can have no practical
bearing on anything outside itself. All literature can by this means be
reduced to the status of a literary exercise. Writers are removed from the
necessary public conversation about matters of importance, are penned
within the university like animals in a feedlot, while their work is learnedly
treated as a subject for specialists. The history of the reading of *I'll Take My
Stand* is a pretty frightening example of the way the departmented university can influence public discourse and communal meaning.

And so the objections to any serious consideration of "A Statement of Principles" can readily be anticipated: It is a literary work and therefore irrelevant; some of its authors did not maintain the stand they took; some of its
authors were then or were always racists. I believe that these objections are
answerable, and I would like to answer them.

The first question to be disposed of is that of credentials: By what authority did the Twelve Southerners presume to speak of agrarianism, industrialism, economy, or any other subject outside of literature? They were, in
truth, a group of writers, intellectuals, and teachers whose paramount experience was certainly not of the workaday world. However, at least three of
them—Lytle, Lanier, and Owsley—had some direct acquaintance with
farming. And all of them, I believe, grew up in circumstances that permitted observation of the countryside and rural life. Their knowledge of agriculture certainly was not as close or complete as one might wish, and yet
they knew better, instinctively and by experience, than to make the great
mistake of the industrialists and the present-day advocates of so-called
global economy and global culture. That is, they never for a moment sup-

posed that a homogeneous technology, methodology, and economy could be undestructively applied to the world's incalculable diversity of climates, topographies, soils, and social conditions.

The great contribution of *I'll Take My Stand*, therefore, is in its astute and uncompromising regionalism. The Twelve Southerners were correct, and virtually alone at the time, in their insistence upon the importance of the local. Their thinking, which stood (and still stands) opposed to that of the agri-industrialists, is perfectly conformable to the thinking of such agricultural scientists as Sir Albert Howard and Wes Jackson, whose guiding principle is that of harmony between local ways of farming and local ecosystems. An agriculture, thus, is good, not by virtue of its universal applicability, but according to its ability to adapt to local conditions and needs. A culture is good according to its ability to provide good local solutions to local problems.

If the initiative of the Southern Agrarians had been supported by similar initiatives in other regions, making their hoped-for "national agrarian movement," then we might have saved much of tangible value and much knowledge that we have now lost. For the relevance of "A Statement of Principles" has been tragically proven by the history subsequent to its publication. In that brief time, we have virtually destroyed the farming population (all the races thereof) along with an enormous amount of farmland. In 1930, the year *I'll Take My Stand* was published, there were about thirty million farmers in this country; at present there are about four million. The farming class is now one of the most despised and most damaged American minorities and has very nearly ceased to exist. By ruin of farmers and rural communities, by erosion, pollution, and various kinds of industrial and urban development, we have ominously degraded and reduced the long-term food-producing capacity of our country. We have done this by our adherence to the industrial principles that have been dominant since the Civil War. I—or any wakeful member of a country community—can show you the gullies, the empty houses, the collapsing barns in the countryside, and the dead main streets of country towns. The World Resources Institute estimates that the net operating income of a Pennsylvania corn and soybean farmer would be reduced by 55 percent if soil depreciation were to be considered a cost of production. You can think your way into the implications of that as far as you can bear to go.

Does it matter that all of the Twelve Southerners who took their stand in 1930 did not remain standing until the benediction? *How* could it matter? They did not invent the principles they stood on, nor were they the first to be anxious about the effects of industrialism. I have known a good many agrarians who stood until they died on agrarian principles, and who never had heard of any of the Twelve Southerners. The only pertinent (or interesting) question is about the correctness of the principles. Ransom's opinion on this matter was, in fact, strenuously disputed by several of his coauthors. Allen Tate, for one, wrote in 1952 that "I have not changed any of my views on Agrarianism since the appearance of *I'll Take My Stand....* I never thought of Agrarianism as a restoration of anything in the Old South; I saw it as something to be created, as I think it will in the long run be created as the result of a profound change . . . in the moral and religious outlook of western man." And Lyle Lanier said in 1980, "I think it's fair to say that *I'll Take My Stand* is a gross understatement of the conditions we face today."

Is "A Statement of Principles" a racist document? I cannot see that it is. Is it racist by association, in the sense that some racists have subscribed to it? I suppose so, but in that case so are the Declaration of Independence, the Constitution of the United States, and the Gospels. Are we going to disown our forebears entirely because partly they were sinners? (Are we willing to stand judgment before our own descendants on the same terms?)

Is an agrarian society necessarily a racist society? I don't think so. In 1930 the most successful agrarian communities in the United States were probably those of the Midwest, which did not depend on the labor of any subject or oppressed race. At that time, moreover, the farmland of the Midwest was distributed more democratically, and was better farmed, than it has been under the dominance of industrial agriculture.

Has the industrialization of American agriculture been good for black people? It undoubtedly has permitted some blacks, like some whites, to make more money. Undoubtedly some, who in 1930 would have been hired hands or sharecroppers or small farmers, in 1999 are making "good money" or even "big money" in industry and the professions. But how much of this gain is net is not clear. The costs certainly have been great. I don't know that we have asked, let alone answered, whether it is better to be a black small farmer in the South or homeless, addicted, jailed, or dead in San Francisco.

"A Statement of Principles" is correct in noticing that "a fresh labor-saving device introduced into an industry does not emancipate the laborers in that industry so much as it evicts them." An industrial economy *profits* (though, of course, only up to a point) from joblessness, which drives down the cost of labor. The chairman and CEO of General Electric made (in salary, bonuses, and stock options) $30 million in 1996—his salary and bonuses having increased by about 20 percent over the preceding year. His main job at that time was to oppose his workers' demands for wage increases. To industrial conservatives, everybody (except themselves) is expendable. To industrial liberals, those expended are adequately compensated by welfare and politically correct terminology. But how much displacement and unemployment is "a good job" worth? Between 1920 and 1988 the number of farms owned by black American farmers declined from 916,000, totaling fifteen million acres, to 30,000, totaling about three million acres. The number of such farms in Mississippi declined from 164,000 in 1910 to fewer than 9,000 in 1980. I don't know what happened to those displaced black landowners, but who would like to assure me that they exchanged their farms for commensurate equity in the industrial system? No "liberal" of any consequence has spoken for those farmers or done anything to help them—and for the most ironic of reasons: because to have done so would have required helping white small farmers as well. And of course no "conservatives" have exerted themselves to help any farmer describable as "small." The reduction of the farm population (black and white) has been a joint project of industrial liberals and industrial conservatives. Is there any evidence that agriculture has been improved by this reduction? Not a shred. The only consequent improvement has been in the profit margins of "agri-industrial" corporations—profits to a considerable extent extracted from the *farm* economy, which has been almost customarily depressed for several decades.

In agriculture, industrialization has dispersed—and, by increasing scale, destroyed the efficacy of—the labor force of farm families and farm neighborhoods. This has caused seasonal labor vacuums, which are now filled by the labor of Mexican and Central American migrants. Dependable numbers are not available, since these people typically are not found by census takers, but Rick Mines of the United States Department of Labor estimates that over the course of a year 2.5 million seasonal or migrant workers are employed on this nation's farms at a yearly income of $5,000 to $7,500, and that three-quarters of these are foreign born. These workers move from one temporary job to another, usually separated from their families, and doing hard work of a kind that modern-day Americans are taught to despise; they earn low wages; they have no connection to the communities in which they work; they have no hope of owning the land on which they work; they have no social or cultural ties to the people for whom they work. As they appear to be infinitely replaceable (more keep coming), they appear also to be infinitely expendable; they have not even the value, and the implied protections, of property. We ought to ask, I suggest, if this is acceptable in a nation still somewhat proud of having freed its slaves. We ought to ask if this is an acceptable way to treat people anywhere, under any circumstances. But beyond those questions lie two others, equally serious: Is this the best way to farm? Is it the best way to keep eating?

It is a fact, unacknowledged but obvious, that for a long time agriculture has been understood by some and (ignorantly or not) accepted by many others as an industry deliberately exploitive not only of land and other natural resources but also of people. In the United States it has exploited black slaves and indentured servants, black and white sharecroppers or tenant farmers, small farmers and landowners, larger industrialized farmers, Mexican and other immigrant laborers. It has depended on people inured to hard work, difficult living conditions, and debt. The world is increasingly filled with people who cannot or will not feed themselves, who therefore must be fed. Farming and land husbandry is therefore work that is not only necessary but increasingly urgent in its importance. And this vital work is so poorly paid that our own people—our own *young* people—do not want to do it or cannot afford to do it. It is work that increasingly we pay Third-World immigrants or Third-World residents to do for us, but which we pay nobody to do well.

The last dog, however, is not yet dead, and Allen Tate may turn out to have been a better prophet than John Crowe Ransom. Tate took his stand and remained standing, seeing correctly that a profound change was needed. Now, more than seven decades after the publication of *I'll Take My Stand*, there is strong evidence that such a change has begun. The agrarian agenda is still in effect; it is well understood and supported by a large and rapidly increasing number of people. Scattered over the United States are hundreds of organizations, large and small, that are working regionally or locally for land conservation, better farming practices, community preservation, local marketing of food and other farm products, preservation of agricultural breeds and varieties, better standards of health, and so on. These people have decided quite consciously and competently, and without the help of their political leaders or appointed experts, that they do not want the world to be owned, all its standards set, and its future decided by a handful of global corporations. Several of the Twelve Southerners, were they alive today, would agree, and would be pleased.

(1999)

Conservationist and Agrarian

I AM A CONSERVATIONIST and a farmer, a wilderness advocate and an agrarian. I am in favor of the world's wildness, not only because I like it, but also because I think it is necessary to the world's life and to our own. For the same reason, I want to preserve the natural health and integrity of the world's economic landscapes, which is to say that I want the world's farmers, ranchers, and foresters to live in stable, locally adapted, resource-preserving communities, and I want them to thrive.

One thing that this means is that I have spent my life on two losing sides. As long as I have been conscious, the great causes of agrarianism and conservation, despite local victories, have suffered an accumulation of losses, some of them probably irreparable—while the third side, that of the land-exploiting corporations, has appeared to grow ever richer. I say "appeared" because I think their wealth is illusory. Their capitalism is based, finally, not on the resources of nature, which it is recklessly destroying, but on fantasy. Not long ago I heard an economist say, "If the consumer ever stops living beyond his means, we'll have a recession." And so the two sides of nature and the rural communities are being defeated by a third side that will eventually be found to have defeated itself.

Perhaps in order to survive its inherent absurdity, the third side is asserting its power as never before: by its control of politics, of public education, and of the news media; by its dominance of science; and by biotechnology, which it is commercializing with unprecedented haste and aggression in order to control totally the world's land-using economies and its food supply. This massive ascendancy of corporate power over democratic process is probably the most ominous development since the end of World War II, and for the most part "the free world" seems to be regarding it as merely normal.

My sorrow in having been for so long on two losing sides has been compounded by knowing that those two sides have been in conflict, not only with their common enemy, the third side, but also, and by now almost conventionally, with each other. And I am further aggrieved in understanding that everybody on my two sides is deeply implicated in the sins and in the fate of the self-destructive third side.

As a part of my own effort to think better, I decided not long ago that I would not endorse any more wilderness preservation projects that do not seek also to improve the health of the surrounding economic landscapes and human communities. One of my reasons is that I don't think we can preserve either wildness or wilderness areas if we can't preserve the economic landscapes and the people who use them. This has put me into discomfort with some of my conservation friends, but that discomfort only balances the discomfort I feel when farmers or ranchers identify me as an "environmentalist," both because I dislike the term and because I sympathize with farmers and ranchers.

Whatever its difficulties, my decision to cooperate no longer in the separation of the wild and the domestic has helped me to see more clearly the compatibility and even the coherence of my two allegiances. The dualism of domestic and wild is, after all, mostly false, and it is misleading. It has obscured for us the domesticity of the wild creatures. More important, it has obscured the absolute dependence of human domesticity upon the wildness that supports it and in fact permeates it. In suffering the now-common accusation that humans are "anthropocentric" (ugly word), we forget that the wild sheep and the wild wolves are respectively ovicentric and lupocentric. The world, we may say, is wild, and all the creatures are homemakers within it, practicing domesticity: mating, raising young, seeking food and comfort. Likewise, though the wild sheep and the farm-bred sheep are in some ways unlike in their domesticities, we forget too easily that if the "domestic" sheep becomes too unwild, as some occasionally do, they become uneconomic and useless: They have reproductive problems, conformation problems, and so on. Domesticity and wildness are in fact intimately connected. What is utterly alien to both is corporate industrialism—a displaced economic life that is without affection for the places where it is lived and without respect for the materials it uses.

The question we must deal with is not whether the domestic and the wild are separate or can be separated; it is how, in the human economy, their indissoluble and necessary connection can be properly maintained.

But to say that wildness and domesticity are not separate, and that we humans are to a large extent responsible for the proper maintenance of their relationship, is to come under a heavy responsibility to be practical. I have two thoroughly practical questions on my mind.

∽

The first is: Why should conservationists have a positive interest in, for example, farming? There are lots of reasons, but the plainest is: Conservationists eat. To be interested in food but not in food production is clearly absurd. Urban conservationists may feel entitled to be unconcerned about food production because they are not farmers. But they can't be let off so easily, for they all are farming by proxy. They can eat only if land is farmed on their behalf by somebody somewhere in some fashion. If conservationists will attempt to resume responsibility for their need to eat, they will be led back fairly directly to all their previous concerns for the welfare of nature.

Do conservationists, then, wish to eat well or poorly? Would they like their food supply to be secure from one year to the next? Would they like their food to be free of poisons, antibiotics, alien genes, and other contaminants? Would they like a significant portion of it to be fresh? Would they like it to come to them at the lowest possible ecological cost? The answers, if responsibly given, will influence production, will influence land use, will determine the configuration and the health of landscapes.

If conservationists merely eat whatever the supermarket provides and the government allows, they are giving economic support to all-out industrial food production; to animal factories; to the depletion of soil, rivers, and aquifers; to crop monocultures and the consequent losses of biological and genetic diversity; to the pollution, toxicity, and overmedication that are the inevitable accompaniments of all-out industrial food production; to a food system based on long-distance transportation and the consequent waste of petroleum and the spread of pests and diseases; and to the division of the countryside into ever-larger farms and ever-larger fields receiving always less human affection and human care.

If, on the other hand, conservationists are willing to insist on having the best food, produced in the best way, as close to their homes as possible, and if they are willing to learn to judge the quality of food and food production, then they are going to give economic support to an entirely different kind of land use in an entirely different landscape. This landscape will have a higher ratio of caretakers to acres, of care to use. It will be at once more domestic and more wild than the industrial landscape. Can increasing the number of farms and farmers in an agricultural landscape enhance the quality of that landscape as wildlife habitat? Can it increase what we might call the wilderness value of that landscape? It *can* do so, and the determining factor would be diversity. Don't forget that we are talking about a landscape that is changing in response to an increase in local consumer demand for local food. Imagine a modern agricultural landscape devoted mainly to corn and soybeans and to animal factories. And then imagine its neighboring city developing a demand for good, locally grown food. To meet that demand, local farming would have to diversify.

If that demand is serious, if it is taken seriously, if it comes from informed and permanently committed consumers, if it promises the necessary economic support, then that radically oversimplified landscape will change. The crop monocultures and animal factories will give way to the mixed farming of plants and animals. Pastured flocks and herds of meat animals, dairy herds, and poultry flocks will return, requiring, of course, pastures and hayfields. If the urban consumers would extend their competent concern for the farming economy to include the forest economy and its diversity of products, that would improve the quality and care, and increase the acreage, of farm woodlands. And we should not forget the possibility that good farmers might, for their own instruction and pleasure, preserve patches of woodland unused. As the meadows and woodlands flourished in the landscape, so would the wild birds and animals. The acreages devoted to corn and soybeans, grown principally as livestock feed or as raw materials for industry, would diminish in favor of the fruits and vegetables required by human dinner tables.

As the acreage under perennial cover increased, soil erosion would decrease and the water-holding capacity of the soil would increase. Creeks and rivers would grow cleaner and their flow more constant. As farms diversified, they would tend to become smaller because complexity and work increase with diversity, and so the landscape would acquire more owners. As the number of farmers and the diversity of their farms increased, the toxicity of agriculture would decrease—insofar as agricultural chemicals are used to replace labor and to defray the biological costs of monoculture. As food production became decentralized, animal wastes would be dispersed, and would be absorbed and retained in the soil as nutrients rather than flowing away as waste and as pollutants. The details of such a transformation could be elaborated almost endlessly. To make short work of it here, we could just say that a dangerously oversimplified landscape would become healthfully complex, both economically and ecologically.

Moreover, since we are talking about a city that would be living in large measure from its local fields and forests, we are talking also about a local economy of decentralized, small, nonpolluting value-adding factories and shops that would be scaled to fit into the landscape with the least ecological or social disruption. And thus we can also credit to this economy an increase in independent small businesses, in self-employment, and a decrease in the combustible fuel needed for transportation and (I believe) for production.

Such an economy is technically possible, there can be no doubt of that; we have the necessary methods and equipment. The capacity of nature to accommodate, and even to cooperate in, such an economy is also undoubtable; we have the necessary historical examples. This is not, from nature's point of view, a pipe dream.

What *is* doubtable, or at least unproven, is the capacity of modern humans to choose, make, and maintain such an economy. For at least half a century we have taken for granted that the methods of farming could safely be determined by the mechanisms of industry, and that the economies of farming could safely be determined by the economic interests of industrial corporations. We are now running rapidly to the end of the possibility of that assumption. The social, ecological, and even the economic costs have become too great, and the costs are still increasing, all over the world.

Now we must try to envision an agriculture founded, not on mechanical principles, but on the principles of biology and ecology. Sir Albert Howard and Wes Jackson have argued at length for such a change of standards. If you want to farm sustainably, they have told us, then you have got to make your farming conform to the natural laws that govern the local ecosystem. You have got to farm with both plants and animals in as great a diversity as possible, you have got to conserve fertility, recycle wastes, keep the ground covered, and so on. Or, as J. Russell Smith put it seventy years ago, you have got to "fit the farming to the land"—not to the available technology or the market, as important as those considerations are, but to the land. It is necessary, in short, to maintain a proper connection between the domestic and the wild. The paramount standard by which the work is to be judged is the health of the place where the work is done.

But this is not a transformation that we can just drift into, as we drift in and out of fashions, and it is not one that we should wait to be forced into by large-scale ecological breakdown. It won't happen if a lot of people—consumers and producers, city people and country people, conservationists and land users—don't get together deliberately to make it happen.

Those are some of the reasons why conservationists should take an interest in farming and make common cause with good farmers. Now I must get on to the second of my practical questions.

Why should farmers be conservationists? Or maybe I had better ask why *are* good farmers conservationists? The farmer lives and works in the meeting place of nature and the human economy, the place where the need for conservation is most obvious and most urgent. Farmers either fit their farming to their farms, conform to the laws of nature, and keep the natural powers and services intact—or they do not. If they do not, then they increase the ecological deficit that is being charged to the future. (I had better admit that some farmers do increase the ecological deficit, but they are not the farmers I am talking about. I am not asking conservationists to support destructive ways of farming.)

Good farmers, who take seriously their duties as stewards of Creation and of their land's inheritors, contribute to the welfare of society in more ways than society usually acknowledges, or even knows. These farmers produce valuable goods, of course; but they also conserve soil, they conserve water, they conserve wildlife, they conserve open space, they conserve scenery.

All that is merely what farmers *ought* to do. But since our present society's first standard in all things is profit and it loves to dwell on "economic reality," I can't resist a glance at these good farmers in their economic circumstances, for these farmers will be poorly paid for the goods they produce, and for the services they render to conservation they will not be paid at all. Good farmers today may market products of high quality and perform well all the services I have listed, and *still* be unable to afford health insurance, and *still* find themselves mercilessly caricatured in the public media as rural simpletons, hicks, or rednecks. And then they hear the voices of the "economic realists": "Get big or get out. Sell out and go to town. Adapt or die." We have had fifty years of such realism in agriculture, and the result has been more and more large-scale monocultures and factory farms, with their ever larger social and ecological—and ultimately economic—costs.

Why do good farmers farm well for poor pay and work as good stewards of nature for no pay, many of them, moreover, having no hope that their farms will be farmed by their children (for the reasons given) or that they will be farmed by anybody?

Well, I was raised by farmers, have farmed myself, and have in turn raised two farmers—which suggests to me that I may know something about farmers, and also that I don't know very much. But over the years I along with a lot of other people have wondered, "Why do they do it?" Why do farmers farm, given their economic adversities on top of the many frustrations and difficulties normal to farming? And always the answer is: "Love. They must do it for love." Farmers farm for the love of farming. They love to watch and nurture the growth of plants. They love to live in the presence of animals. They love to work outdoors. They love the weather, maybe even when it is making them miserable. They love to live where they work and to work where they live. If the scale of their farming is small enough, they like to work in the company of their children and with the help of their children. They love the measure of independence that farm life can still provide. I have an idea that a lot of farmers have gone to a lot of trouble merely to be self-employed, to live at least a part of their lives without a boss.

And so the first thing farmers as conservationists must try to conserve is their love of farming and their love of independence. Of course they can conserve these things only by handing them down, by passing them on to their children, or to *somebody's* children. Perhaps the most urgent task for all of us who want to eat well and to keep eating is to encourage farm-raised children to take up farming. And we must recognize that this only can be done economically. Farm children are not encouraged by watching their parents take their products to market only to have them stolen at prices less than the cost of production.

But farmers obviously are responsible for conserving much more than agrarian skills and attitudes. I have already told why farmers should be, as much as any conservationists, conservers of the wildness of the world—and that is their inescapable dependence on nature. Good farmers, I believe, recognize a difference that is fundamental between what is natural and what

is man-made. They know that if you treat a farm as a factory and living creatures as machines, or if you tolerate the idea of "engineering" organisms, then
you are on your way to something destructive and, sooner or later, too expensive. To treat creatures as machines is an error with large practical implications.

Good farmers know too that nature can be an economic ally. Natural
fertility is cheaper, often in the short run, always in the long run, than purchased fertility. Natural health, inbred and nurtured, is cheaper than phar-
maceuticals and chemicals. Solar energy—if you know how to capture and
use it: in grass, say, and the bodies of animals—is cheaper than petroleum.
The highly industrialized factory farm is entirely dependent on "purchased
inputs." The agrarian farm, well integrated into the natural systems that
support it, runs to an economically significant extent on resources and supplies that are free.

It is now commonly assumed that when humans took to agriculture they
gave up hunting and gathering. But hunting and gathering remained until
recently an integral and lively part of my own region's traditional farming
life. People hunted for wild game; they fished the ponds and streams; they
gathered wild greens in the spring, hickory nuts and walnuts in the fall;
they picked wild berries and other fruits; they prospected for wild honey.
Some of the most memorable, and least regrettable, nights of my own youth
were spent in coon hunting with farmers. There is no denying that these
activities contributed to the economy of farm households, but a further fact
is that they were pleasures; they were wilderness pleasures, not greatly different from the pleasures pursued by conservationists and wilderness lovers.
As I was always aware, my friends the coon hunters were not motivated
just by the wish to tree coons and listen to hounds and listen to each other,
all of which were sufficiently attractive; they were coon hunters also because
they wanted to be afoot in the woods at night. Most of the farmers I have
known, and certainly the most interesting ones, have had the capacity to
ramble about outdoors for the mere happiness of it, alert to the doings of
the creatures, amused by the sight of a fox catching grasshoppers, or by the
puzzle of wild tracks in the snow.

As the countryside has depopulated and the remaining farmers have
come under greater stress, these wilderness pleasures have fallen away. But
they have not yet been altogether abandoned; they represent something
probably essential to the character of the best farming, and they should be
remembered and revived.

Those, then, are some reasons why good farmers are conservationists, and why all farmers ought to be.

What I have been trying to do is to define a congruity or community of interest between farmers and conservationists who are not farmers. To name the interests that these two groups have in common, and to observe, as I did at the beginning, that they also have common enemies, is to raise a question that is becoming increasingly urgent: Why don't the two groups publicly and forcefully agree on the things they agree on, and make an effort to cooperate? I don't mean to belittle their disagreements, which I acknowledge to be important. Nevertheless, cooperation is now necessary, and it is possible. If Kentucky tobacco farmers can meet with antismoking groups, draw up a set of "core principles" to which they all agree, and then support those principles, something of the sort surely could happen between conservationists and certain land-using enterprises: family farms and ranches, small-scale, locally owned forestry and forest products industries, and perhaps others. Something of the sort, in fact, is beginning to happen, but so far the efforts are too small and too scattered. The larger organizations on both sides need to take an interest and get involved.

If these two sides, which need to cooperate, have so far been at odds, what is the problem? The problem, I think, is economic. The small land-users, on the one hand, are struggling so hard to survive in an economy controlled by the corporations that they are distracted from their own economy's actual basis in nature. They also have not paid enough attention to the difference between their always threatened local economies and the apparently thriving corporate economy that is exploiting them.

On the other hand, the mostly urban conservationists, who mostly are ignorant of the economic adversities of, say, family-scale farming or ranching, have paid far too little attention to the connection between *their* economic life and the despoliation of nature. They have trouble seeing that the bad farming and forestry practices that they oppose as conservationists are done on their behalf, and with their consent implied in the economic proxies they have given as consumers.

These clearly are serious problems. Both of them indicate that the industrial economy is not a true description of economic reality, and moreover that this economy has been wonderfully successful in getting its falsehoods believed. Too many land users and too many conservationists seem to have accepted the doctrine that the availability of goods is determined by the availability of cash, or credit, and by the market. In other words, they have accepted the idea always implicit in the arguments of the land-exploiting corporations: that there can be, and that there is, a safe disconnection between economy and ecology, between human domesticity and the wild world. Industrializing farmers have too readily assumed that the nature of their land could safely be subordinated to the capability of their technology, and that conservation could safely be left to conservationists. Conservationists have too readily assumed that the integrity of the natural world could be preserved mainly by preserving tracts of wilderness, and that the nature and nurture of the economic landscapes could safely be left to agribusiness, the timber industry, debt-ridden farmers and ranchers, and migrant laborers.

To me, it appears that these two sides are as divided as they are because each is clinging to its own version of a common economic error. How can this be corrected? I don't think it can be, so long as each of the two sides remains closed up in its own conversation. I think the two sides need to enter into *one* conversation. They have got to talk to one another. Conservationists have got to know and deal competently with the methods and economics of land use. Land users have got to recognize the urgency, even the economic urgency, of the requirements of conservation.

Failing this, these two sides will simply concede an easy victory to their common enemy, the third side, the corporate totalitarianism which is now rapidly consolidating as "the global economy" and which will utterly dominate both the natural world and its human communities.

(2002)

Tuscany

——————— ❧ ———————

THAT I SHOULD have been asked to speak in Tuscany at a meeting
concerned with food and hunger is appropriate, and it is very moving
to me, because my conscious effort to think about agriculture and its problems began in Tuscany more than forty years ago.

In 1961 and 1962, my wife and daughter and I spent several months in
Florence, learning in the process to speak a dialect of tourist-Italian that I
cannot now reproduce. We lived in a cottage that once had been the barn of
a monastery south of the Arno. I was there on a fellowship intended to
acquaint me with the life and art of a foreign country, which it did. I gathered
much from the streets, shops, churches, gardens, and museums of Florence
that has been useful and dear, never far from my mind, in the years since.

But what I saw here in the Tuscan countryside required me also to begin
to think about agriculture in a way I had not thought about it before. I had
been raised as a farmer and an agrarian. As a young writer, however, I had
learned to think of myself as a person destined to live far from my native
place and the farming life that I had grown up in.

I did not change my mind quickly, but I did change it, and the change
began during those months in Tuscany. We were living on the edge of Florence. From our windows we could see farmers at work with their teams of
white cattle on a terraced slope on which crops of grain stood among olive
trees and grape vines. Reeds and willows growing along the waterways provided stakes for the vines and osiers with which to tie the vines to the stakes.

I had never imagined such farming as this was. I studied it carefully and
with excitement. It was a way of farming that was lovingly adapted to its
place. It was highly diversified. It wasted nothing. It was scaled to permit
close attention to details. It was beautiful. I began to understand that

———————

This is a speech prepared for a meeting at San Rossori at Pisa.

probably the supreme works of art in Tuscany were its agricultural land-scapes.

Another thing I understood was that this great, still contemporary, daily-working work of art was very old. The terraced slopes and small valley fields had been farmed in essentially the same way by essentially the same people for many centuries. Through all that time, these people had performed a continuous act of fidelity to the land, to the seasons, to their crops and animals, and to human need. They had maintained their work and their faithfulness through hardships of every kind.

And so my first visit to Tuscany taught me something of the appearance, the practical means, the meaning, and the value of a way of farming developed in a long association between a local community and its land. I have not ceased to think of these things in the years since. That an agriculture so complexly satisfying—at once elegant, abundant, conserving, and necessary—should have survived for so long was profoundly instructive to me. The memory of it has given me both pleasure and encouragement.

There is of course much to be said about the traditional agriculture of Tuscany, and I don't know enough to say more than a little. But if we know anything of the history of farming anywhere, we know that even so fine an agriculture as this would have been mostly ignored or taken for granted by the people of wealth, power, and influence who were dependent upon it.

I learned, on a second visit in the fall of 1992, that the traditional agriculture I was so fortunate to see only thirty years before had all too expectably given way to industrialization. It will take a long time, I believe, to comprehend and to live out all the implications of this change. Its most immediately visible sign is the shift from the old horizontal cultivation of the slopes, natural to man and beast, to the up-and-down cultivation enabled, and even required, by machines. The resulting soil erosion may be understood as something that inevitably happens when the attention, memory, and affection of the people have been alienated from the land.

I want to be careful not to encourage oversimplification. I am not saying that the old was all good and the new is all bad. Nor am I saying that there is something invariably destructive in the use of industrial machinery in agriculture. And yet it is not wrong to say that we have not thought as carefully as we must think about how and on what scale the machines ought to be used. And it is merely necessary to say that the substitution of industrial standards for agrarian standards in the land economies is a costly mistake.

Industrial standards in agriculture virtually institutionalize, and enforce, the indifference of the general population to the welfare of the land and the people of the land. Under industrialism, the farmers, and especially the smaller farmers, are overworked and underpaid, and this exactly corresponds to the condition of the land under industrialism: Much is taken, little that belongs to it given back. The fertility that is given back most often comes from nonrenewable sources. The organic wastes that should be returned to the fields as fertilizer most often enter streams and rivers as pollutants, as do the excess chemical fertilizers. The work of the industrial economy, we may say, is to transform assets into liabilities.

Industrialism damages agriculture by removing the cultural, economic, and technological constraints that assure propriety of scale. When the scale of work is appropriate to the place where the work is done, then attention, memory, and affection have a consequential power, and our limited human intelligence can be used without extreme or permanent damage. But limited intelligence minus traditional restraints plus unlimited funds equals unlimited damage. Only an appropriately-scaled, locally-adapted, locally-owned economy can make a commonwealth of a "natural resource."

The absolutely critical issue, of course, is that of local adaptation. Our great error has been to learn to think of the world as a collection of nations, when in fact it is a collection of *places*, differing from one another according to climate, soil, daylength, altitude, exposure, drainage, and ecology, as well as cultural demand and economic need. Small places, side by side, can sometimes differ complexly.

The human economy is under an inescapable obligation to adapt itself conservingly to the multiplicity of unique earthly places. There is no impracticality in saying this, because some human economies, and even the economies of some individual farmers, have made this adaptation—never perfectly, to be sure, and with varying success, but they have accepted the obligation, and have made the health of the place the standard of their work.

Recently I heard a good forester say that industrial loggers are interested only in what can be taken out of the forest, but that locally responsible loggers are even more interested in what will be left. This distinction applies to all soil-based economies. In all of them we must choose to treat the soil either as a mine, finally exhaustible, or as the endlessly self-renewing source that it can be with proper care.

Local adaptation happens in nature because of the genetic resourcefulness of species and the uniqueness of individual creatures. The analogous human resources are economic democracy and political liberty. The land must be farmed in small parcels. And because local adaptation is never perfect and never final, but is necessarily a continuous process, people must be free to develop and apply new knowledge, and so correct themselves.

Obviously, an agriculture of any kind is a product of culture. It is equally obvious that bad farming can be a consequence of bad policy or bad politics. The extent to which *good* farming can be a result of political policy is a different question, and it is a troubling one.

Clear as it is that the maintenance or development of good agriculture can be politically obstructed, it is not clear how good agriculture can be the direct result of policy, even of good policy. In view of the almost inconceivable multiplicity and diversity of places, it is hard to see how local adaptation can be the result of central planning. Local adaptation probably can be accomplished only by farmers living and working in stable communities, within adequate local cultures, at peace, over a long time. It may be that governments can serve such a possibility only in negative ways: for example, by preventing great concentrations of wealth, which destroy local cultures and agricultures simply by their inevitable ignorance or indifference. Can power be generous to small places? It can, but only by leaving the people of those places free to use them well.

In earlier times, there were technological limits on the ability of people of wealth and power to exploit agriculture; the land had to be farmed by the land's energy collected in the bodies of humans and animals. The land's people, enslaved or free, were on the land. They had to farm well or die. Often enough, they farmed well enough to live and to keep others alive.

Now, for a while at least, the old limits of handwork and bodily energy have been removed by industrial technology and the fossil fuels. The ability to exploit agriculture has thus been centralized as never before. The great corporations and their political servants are concerned exclusively with "the global economy," which is a euphemism for global colonialism, and with the need to protect it from the violence it provokes. They have not yet decided—but they are going to have to decide—whether the global economy is operating under the protection of global militarism or in conflict with it. In these circumstances, can we expect power to be generous to small places? This is the great practical question that we now face, and we know the answer: Any such expectation would be foolish. If a government's economic responsibilities are defined by the corporate interest, then it can have neither the intention nor the ability to be generous to small places. The corporate interest aims at uniformity, and is therefore incapable of perceiving the value of unique places, creatures, human beings, and human cultures. The global economy is no more discriminating than any other weapon of mass destruction. That is why many of us are working now to develop local economies, partnerships of local producers and local consumers, which are the only effective answer to great concentrations of wealth and power.

Our situation is both comic and tragic. On the one hand, the self-styled "realists" of the corporate economy are unable to conform their thinking to any reality except that of selfishness. The utterly dull and humorless "realism" of the self-absorbed has done what it was bound to do: It has brought absurdity, waste, and ruin to an unprecedented magnitude. It has made violence normal, both as war and as "economic growth."

On the other hand, the opponents of those "realists" have been making for many years an argument that, except in a time perfectly insane, would not need to be made. They are saying that the human economy must achieve some sort of harmony with the economy of nature; that human work must shape itself conservingly within the limits of the natural world and of human intelligence; and that we cannot define or achieve a good economy or do good work within the terms of nationalist belligerence and industrial war. They are saying that to preserve the capacity of every region of the world to sustain its creatures in good health is the real work of peace and of human security. To truths so plain and self-evident, the ears of the realistically selfish are closed.

This, of course, is the description of an emergency. It is moreover an emergency of the worst kind: one that cannot be resolved by "emergency measures." It is an emergency that calls for patience, and to be patient in an emergency is a hard requirement. But patience is what we must have if we hope to complete our work.

Obviously, we must use the emergency measures that are available to us, though there are not many. We must do what we can politically, though our political power at present is not great. But we must remember that good work cannot have a merely political completion. Our work will not be completed in the world's capitals, but in healthful farms and forests, ecosystems and watersheds, and in coherent communities. More important even than political victory for our side is the necessity to keep our thinking sound enough and complex enough to deal effectively with actual problems and needs. We must not let either political urgency or our sense of peril reduce us to the proto-warfare of slogans and sound bites.

I had a dream not long ago that I want to tell you about. I dreamed that the industrialists had at last contrived the ultimate answer to the human longing for flight. They had built an enormous airplane, an aeronautical Tower of Babel. All the world's people who wished to escape the limits of earthly life were invited to take passage, at the cost only of all their earthly rights and properties. In their millions and billions they came aboard, and the plane took off. But two unforeseen circumstances were immediately evident. Even so large a plane could not carry enough fuel to fly indefinitely; sooner or later it would have to land. But the violence of its departure had destroyed the runway. While the escapists circled the globe, free of their ancient limits and restraints, but running out of fuel, a small ground crew worked frantically to rebuild the runway, hoping to bring the wanderers safely down to earth again. My dream did not give the outcome.

I am telling my dream, obviously, because it is an accurate description of the human situation at present. A fantastical, airy economy, proposing to grow infinitely from finite resources, has lifted our species far above its earthly homelands. It is facing not only a limited fuel supply but also the earth's limited ability to endure the burning of the fuel that is left. How to get this economy safely down to earth is our problem.

But my dream also clarifies the point I was just trying to make. If the fantastical airship of the present economy does manage to return to earth with survivors, that will be, on an immensely magnified scale, like the landing of Noah's Ark. The returnees will need careful instructions on how to live again on the earth. That is why we dare not permit our thinking to become too simple or uncritical or impractical. At the end of their dangerous trip, the exiles will need to be invited into an ongoing, vigorous conversation about farming, forestry, local economy, energy, ecology, health, and the domestic arts. Without this conversation and the good work that it calls for, the noblest slogans will not help.

(2003)

Is Life a Miracle?

. . . if he gather unto himself his spirit and his breath;
All flesh shall perish together, and man shall turn again unto dust.

—Job 34: 14–15

Man is a creature created to be the son of God. . . .
Death and corruption are profoundly alien to his nature:
they are profoundly unnatural to him. What is natural to him is precisely
that eternal life which is his through participation in the divine.

—Philip Sherrard, *The Rape of Man and Nature*, p. 27

THERE ARE MANY people who know more than I do about the issues that have concerned me in my essays. I am a man mostly ignorant of the things that are most important to me.

Why then have I presumed to be an essayist?

Because of fear, I think. I write essays to see what I can find in myself with which to answer the terrifying fact of the human destructiveness of good things. And I write as a would-be free person, trying to fight shy of the official, the commercial, and the fashionable.

My resources are the things in my cultural inheritance that I have recognized as my own and have tried to live up to: agrarianism, democracy, and Christianity. I believe:

1. That good farming and good forestry are fundamental goods, for those who do the work and for those for whom the work is done.

2. That it is wrong for people to be excluded from decisions that affect their lives.

3. That every thing that exists is a divine gift, which places us in a position of extreme danger, solvable only by love for everything that exists, including our enemies.

When one receives a divine gift, one must be glad of it; one must be grateful for it; one must take care of it.

The obligation of giving care, of returning stewardship for gifts, calls us to be responsible heirs of another birthright of culture: good art. I use the word "art" in its broadest and truest sense: a way of making, not only the works of the so-called fine arts, but all the other things we need as well. I mean, for examples, the arts of food, clothing, and shelter.

To make things in a way that answers the requirements of good steward-ship requires both good artistry and great breadth of mind. It requires a mind capable of seeing human work within its various contexts: religious, ecolog-ical, economic, cultural, and political. The modern, specialist mind makes things badly, by the measures of stewardship, of artistry, and often even of utility. It is a mind too narrow, and its artistry is incomplete and destructive.

I have not written essays such as *Life Is a Miracle,* I must say, in self-defense, for it is clear to me that I have not measured up to the requirements I have submitted to. But I have written them, certainly, in defense of the requirements, and to keep myself reminded of what those requirements immemorially are.

In the year 2000, I published a small book, *Life Is a Miracle.* My friend Charlie Sing has now asked me to deal with the question "Is life a mira-cle?"—thus inviting me to defend my title. Did I really mean it?

Yes, I did, and I do, mean it. And I mean it practically. I know that humans, including modern biologists, have learned a good deal about liv-ing things, and about parts of living things. But I don't believe that anybody knows much about the *life* of living things. I have seen with my own eyes and felt with my own hands many times the difference between live things and dead ones, and I do not believe that the difference can be so explained as to remove the wonder from it. What is the coherence, the integrity, the consciousness, the intelligence, the spirit, the informing form that leaves a living body when it dies? What was the "green fire" that Aldo Leopold saw going out in the eyes of the dying wolf? When you watch the eyes of the dying there comes a moment when you *see* that they no longer see. I think a great painter can paint the difference between an eye that is dead and a living eye, but I don't think anybody can *explain* the difference except by an infinite regression of responses to an infinitely repeated question: "But what was the cause of *that* cause?"

To me, as a matter of principle and of belief, life is a miracle. I so believe because life is more credible to me as a miracle than it is as an accident or as somebody's property. "Miracle" is a word that encompasses more of what I have experienced of life than do other words more frequently applied to it.

But my belief is not the practical point. The practical point is that *if* I believe life is a miracle, I will grant it a respect and a deference that I would not grant it otherwise. If I believe it is a miracle, then I cannot believe that I am superior to it, or that I understand it, or that I own it.

Perhaps I will have to submit to somewhat the same result if I believe merely that I can't know for sure that life is *not* a miracle. In either case, I am granting to life, and to each living thing, its own inherent dignity and mystery.

In the context of this issue, dignity and mystery function virtually as synonyms. For without its mystery a creature can have no dignity. The presumption of complete understanding is always an affront to dignity. So is the presumption that complete understanding will eventually be realized, or that it is not realizable *yet*. Every creature has an inherent right not to be completely understood. That is the basis of its freedom.

The analogy between creatures and machines or minds and computers is invariably offensive because it offers an imperfect likeness as a complete explanation. It is blindness to fail to see—and hubris of the most dangerous sort to refuse to see—the difference between a thing and any other thing to which it may be compared, or the difference between a thing and its explanation.

A machine may or may not be able to perform work resembling that of "human cognition"—that is a problem beyond my competence. But I suspect that the term "cognition" itself involves an oversimplification of the actual life and work of a mind. And I know that no machine could perform work resembling that of Paul Cézanne or any good farmer, because the work of both presupposes a specifically human life's devotion both to the practice of an art and to love for a specific landscape. Cézanne said, "Were it not that I am passionately fond of the contours of my country, I should not be here."

To say that life is a miracle, then, is to insist upon the uniqueness and the unique value of individual creatures; it is to set creatures free from generalizations about them. Some time ago I received a letter from New Mexico that offered the following dialogue:

"How do you train horses?"

"Which one do you have in mind?"

I would accept that as a pretty adequate summary of my essay *Life Is a Miracle*.

Each of the world's innumerable creatures is unique, and each of the world's innumerable places is unique. Creatures survive in their places by local adaptation. To believe these things is to see that we must not separate ourselves too far from nature. We must learn to live a given life in a given world. Our ability to change either our life or our place is limited. To transgress those limits is to put ourselves and our places in danger. Now we are faced with a choice between life as defined by the corporate economy and its client institutions, including governments, and life as defined by our own nature and the nature of our home landscapes—between life as a commodity and life as an unreproducible gift, as what I think is properly called a miracle. Life as a miracle is a gift to be accepted. Its acceptance implicates us in gratitude, and in a responsibility of care that is fearful, difficult, and yet pleasing. This is the only antidote I know to the ideas of life as commodity, as property, or as subject.

To say that life is a miracle is to say that it is a commonwealth, which to possess is to share with all other creatures. It is not a commonwealth of the living only. A living mind is a member of a commonwealth that includes the dead, just as the living embodiments of the soil, from humans to microorganisms, live by participation in the commonwealth of all their ancestry. The process by which each single life is prepared by so many lives and so many deaths has not been comprehended by any human mind, and no human mind is ever going to comprehend it. But to recognize that this commonwealth exists is to be moved immediately beyond the dualisms of humanity and nature by which some justify their destruction of nature and others justify preserving nature merely as "wilderness."

To say that life is a miracle is to insist that life is not exclusively the concern of science and commerce, but is also, and *still* legitimately, the concern of religion, politics, and the arts—as appropriately and as needfully to be dealt with by prayer or policy or music or farming as by experimentation and trade.

To say that life is a miracle is thus a restoration of language. If I have called life a miracle, that is because I am trying to find a language that can keep us whole enough and humble enough to preserve the world and stay alive. We need that word "miracle," honestly used, as we need all the rest of our words, but we need this one especially, as a part of the language of sanctity that we have come so near to losing. By speaking this word "miracle" we call back into our conversation about life, not only the practitioners of disciplines other than biology, but also our guides and fellow members from the past. Why in our destructive and anxious age should not biologists, politicians, artists (and even professors of literature) interest themselves in the Bible's understanding of life as a divine gift and sacred trust, or in the moral structure of the landscapes of Shakespeare and Andrew Marvell, or in Milton's dealing with the problem of freedom and obedience? Such practical reading is now virtually forbidden in our schools, but it would restore indispensable voices to our conversation.

To say that life is a miracle is to pry open the now dominant and conventional discourse of materialism to admit nonmaterial realities. It is easy to be amused at the materialists who, insisting upon the exclusive realness of materials, fail to see that "materialism" is an idea, having no more materiality than any other idea. They fail to see the utter instantaneousness and transitoriness of the material world and the huge component of nonmateriality of which human life is made. We have our material existence only in the unstoppable, nearly unthinkable flux of the present. The past, which apparently is real enough even to materialists, does not exist except in immaterial thoughts and memories. (If the past had material existence, there would be far fewer quarrels among historians.) The future, to which some materialists assign immoderate value, is merely a projection or speculation, less substantial, as having fewer witnesses, than that faith which is "the evidence of things not seen."

❧

I wrote parts of this essay while sitting in a boat tied up in the shade along the bank of the Kentucky River. What I was doing, besides writing, was watching the swallows. The swallows—martins, barn swallows, and rough-wings—love the river and they are always in flight over it, feeding, drinking, bathing, and (I am sure) enjoying themselves. I have no trouble in understanding that every swallow has a form, flight, voice, and life history that is characteristic of its species. But, watching, I see also that every swallow is unrepeatably what it is in each moment. We watch swallows with fascination because of our intuition that no swallow ever does twice quite the same thing that it or any other swallow has ever done. And this is because the swallows are living.

The swallows are living, as we know, only because all the rest of the world's living creatures are living in a world that is alive. They are all only now, only instantaneously, living. This is an immense fact. It will never be fully recorded by any human. It will never be fully comprehended by any human mind. It is certainly a great mystery. In calling it a miracle, if I am incorrect, I am at least safe from correction.

But now, out of courtesy to theoretical possibility, I will ask, Is it not theoretically possible that someday there will be a computer capable of gathering all the data of this great living in one of its moments, plotting the formality of its many motions and relationships, from that construing its indwelling principle of coherence, and so proving at last that life is or is not a miracle?

When that question first occurred to me, I thought I was going to have to say that, yes, such a thing is theoretically possible. But, after reflection, I have decided that the answer must be no. The reason is that we are dealing here with time and the experience of life in time. Though experience may, within limits, be reducible to explanations or even to laws, it cannot be reproduced—not by the swallows, not by us. Those of us who have grown up recognize the idea of the reproduction of experience as an adolescent fantasy: Last Saturday's wonderful party is not going to happen again this Saturday, for time has passed, history has continued, and we are older. By the time it occurs to us to gather the data of a moment, the moment is already beyond reach. This moment becomes that moment before we can quite perceive or articulate the change, let alone gather any data. We are alive *only* in the present moment, not in the previous moment or the following one. We can, at least theoretically, inventory the entire contents of a space, but we cannot even conceivably inventory the entire contents of a moment in time. It is a little as though we have undertaken to learn about a ghost by following its tracks. This does happen to be a ghost that leaves physically present and examinable tracks, but it is nonetheless a ghost. We have filled libraries with records tracing the way it has gone, but we do not appear to be gaining on it.

The difficulty of understanding the instantaneity of life is this. It is clear that we are alive only in the present, not in the past or in the future. The present, we assume, is "the time" in which we are alive. But how long a time is it? We see immediately that we must say, "Not very long."

But *exactly* how long is it? There is the difficulty. Past and future never overlap. And they are, it seems, very close together. The time between them we conceive to be "the present." The present seems to be the interval in which the future pours itself into the past. But how long is this interval? Does it have a measurable length? Does it, in any verifiable way, exist?

The shortest conceivable time—a nanosecond, say—has duration. It has a time when it begins and a time when it ends. In the course of its duration, it has a future, a present, and a past, just as does a footrace or a construction job. But the length of the activity doesn't increase the length of the present.

We have to conclude that the present, for all practical purposes, is immeasurably short. If it is immeasurably short, is it therefore metaphysical? We have to say at least that it *probably* is. (We are talking, to begin with, about the measurement of time, which, of itself, has no physical existence.)

Zeno's smaller and smaller slicings of distance affront common sense. We know that Achilles will quickly overtake the tortoise, simply by striding across the infinitely fractionable space that divides them. And it is evident too that space is a measurable quantity, whatever the length of the unit of measurement.

But our failure to measure the length of the living present does not affront common sense. It is a clue to something both real and immeasurable in our experience. We know that the present exists, because we know that life exists, but we can't find its measure; we can't prove its existence. Here is where empiricism fails and experience forever eludes experimentation.

If eternity is "now" as well as "forever," does it not follow that this elusive present tense of life is eternal, and that physical life is (as in my epigraphs from the Book of Job and Philip Sherrard) a participation in, or of, God's life? I suppose that this is an article of faith, necessarily. But it can't be empirically disproven.

If this argument holds (and my faith in argument is limited), it is rich in implications, one of which certainly is our freedom from reductionist materialism.

The practical problem, in short, is that life is instantaneous but we can deal with it only in terms of duration, and in our dealing we are always, by necessity, a little late. This is the dilemma and the tragedy of life in time, and our computers, no matter how capacious or fast, are there with us.

But even supposing that an omniscient and extratemporal computer might be possible, I believe that its possibility is utterly irrelevant. What is relevant is that we humans are part of a life that is possible only because all living things have it somehow in common, and we do not, we probably cannot, understand how it works. We are not superior to it, we cannot in any final sense own or control it, we cannot fully appreciate it, we cannot be grateful enough for it. It is *ourselves,* not our machines, who must recognize its beauty, its preciousness, and its mystery. If we don't, we won't take care of it. We will destroy it.

I could say, I suppose, that a part of my purpose in *Life Is a Miracle* was to try to put science in its place. It offends and frightens me that some people now evidently believe that the long human conversation about life will sooner or later be conducted exclusively by scientists. This offends me because I believe it rests upon a falsehood. It frightens me because I believe that such falsehoods—the falsehoods of radical oversimplification—damage life and threaten to destroy it.

I think, of course, that science has a place, but I don't think it has a superior place. To start with, I don't think science is superior to any of its subjects—not to the merest laboratory mouse. I don't think *any* art or scholarly discipline is superior to its subject. The human conversation has had moments of light—light, always, is potential in it—and yet it is a conversation conducted mostly in the dark. It is a conversation limited by human limits, a conversation that is or ought to be humble, because it is humbling, full of bewilderment and trouble. It is not going to be ended by anybody's discovery of some ultimate fact.

Science is not superior to its subjects, nor is it inherently superior to the other disciplines. It becomes markedly inferior when it becomes grandiose in its own estimate of itself. In my opinion, science falsifies itself by seeing itself either as a system for the production of marketable ideas or as a romantic quest for some definitive "truth of the universe." It would do far better to understand itself as a part of a highly diverse effort of human thought, never to be completed, that might actually have the power to make us kinder to one another and to our world.

And so I think that science has its proper and necessary place in a conversation with all the other disciplines, all being equal members, with equal time to talk, and no discipline talking ever except to all the others, whatever the market in "jobs" or "intellectual property," so that our whole humanity, in all its parts and concerns, might speak and be spoken for in the one meeting—which we could call, maybe, if we had it, a university.

(2002)